The
Family
Man

THE FAMILY MAN

Todd Strasser

F
STR
C.1

St. Martin's Press
NEW YORK

Library of Congress Cataloging-in-Publication Data

Strasser, Todd.
   The family man / by Todd Strasser.
   p. cm.
   ISBN 0-312-01427-9
   I. Title.
PS3569. T69132F3 1988   87-27958
813'.54—dc 19   CIP

First Edition

10 9 8 7 6 5 4 3 2 1

For Lia, someday.

PART ONE

1

S TUART Miller stood by the French doors of his new
apartment, gazing down at the city street below.
Cars and yellow cabs raced by. A blond woman
wearing lavender shorts and a white T-shirt jogged past a
super washing down the sidewalk with a hose. At the curb,
half a dozen pigeons pecked a half-eaten bagel to bits.

Stuart reached into his pants pocket and pulled out a
handkerchief, which he used to pat his forehead. It was a
hot day, unusually humid for May, and he had gotten up
from his new ergonomic office chair to unstick his cotton
shirt from his back. The new chair was in the office of his
new apartment, from which he had, just that morning,
commenced to run his new business. As he stood by the
doors he reflected proudly upon the fact that he was, for the
first time in his life, his own boss. And not only that, but he
was working out of his own house. Considering the tax
advantages and the fact that he had accomplished this by the
age of thirty-four, he was rather pleased with himself.

A slight movement in the hotel across the street caught
his eye. Stuart glanced up to the ninth floor at a window,

unadorned by curtains or shades. It looked dark inside and he wondered if it was only a chance reflection of sunlight through the thin gray clouds that had caught his attention.

His eyes traveled down the grimy beige facade of the hotel to the torn green awning with EXCELSIOR ARMS printed in dull gold script on the side. A large wooden plaque near the entrance proclaimed that it provided furnished one- and one-and-a-half-room apartments on a weekly or monthly basis. On an otherwise attractive block of well-kept fourteen-story prewar co-ops, the Excelsior Arms was an eyesore, rumored to be populated by prostitutes and drug addicts. Stuart and his wife, Laurie, had eyed it nervously during their first visit to the apartment.

"If you want sterility, look on the East Side," the real-estate agent had said.

Stuart and Laurie had agreed they didn't want sterility. On the other hand, they weren't certain how unsterile they wanted to get, either. What had really attracted them to the apartment was its West End Avenue location, a residential avenue, not some busy street lined with shops, a place where their two-year-old daughter Claire could grow up unharassed by the city's frantic pace. And so, with only minor trepidation, they bought the apartment and accepted a little unsterility in their lives.

Stuart tucked the handkerchief back into his pants pocket. A man from the local discount appliance store was supposed to come by that afternoon and give him a quote on having air conditioners installed. Not that the cost really mattered. He would be spending eight or nine hours a day in this room and he wasn't about to sweat all summer.

Something moved again in the room on the ninth floor across the street. Stuart looked up and saw that a young woman wearing a white robe had come to the window. Her hair was thick and dark and fell past her shoulders. She appeared attractive. For some reason her features made him think she was Spanish or South American or wherever Bianca Jagger had originally come from.

4

She yawned and lifted a hand to cover her mouth. As she did, two thoughts struck Stuart simultaneously. One was that it was nearly three in the afternoon and yet it seemed that she had just woken up. The other was that her robe was neither belted nor buttoned in front. As she lifted her arm it fell open slightly, revealing the shapely curve of her bosom.

Just then, the new four-line speakerphone on his desk emitted its high-pitched tweet. Reluctantly, he stepped away from the French doors and answered it.

"Stuart?" It was his mother.

"Hi, Mom."

"This is your first day working at home?"

"Yup." He sat down and tilted his chair back, resting his feet on the corner of his desk.

"How do you like it?"

"Fine so far."

"Not too lonely?"

Stuart glanced back at the French doors. From his desk he could not see the woman's room. "Nope."

"Good. And how is my darling granddaughter?"

"Fine."

"I don't think a day-care center is right for a child her age."

"We want to give it a try, Mom. I'll be close by if there's a problem."

"And how is your wife?"

"Her name is Laurie."

"Yes, I know."

"She's fine."

"All right," his mother said. "Let's get down to business. Have you got the latest issue of *New York* magazine there?"

"I think so, why?"

"Get it."

"What do you need?" he asked.

"Just get it," she said.

He put the phone down and went back to look at the

5

woman across the street, expecting to find her gone from sight. Instead, she had opened her window and was leaning out, her hands planted firmly on the sill, elbows locked, her face tilted upward and her eyes closed. Stuart blinked. Her robe had fallen open and her medium-sized breasts were bared to the hot air for all the avenue to see.

"Unbelievable," he muttered, quickly glancing down at the sidewalk to see if anyone had stopped to watch. A mother in a yellow sundress pushed a baby stroller and pulled a dog on a leash. A black kid pedaled a D'Agostino delivery bike. A man in a tan suit walked by carrying a briefcase. None of them noticed the naked woman nine stories above.

Stuart looked at her again, feeling both fascinated and uneasy. Like most New Yorkers, he was accustomed to seeing the unusual, but *how could she do that*? Wouldn't she know, or at least suspect, that someone might be watching?

Then he remembered his mother and went into the living room to find the most recent *New York*.

When he returned, the woman across the street was gone. He picked up the phone.

"That took you long enough."

"I wasn't sure where it was," he said.

"Turn to page sixty-six," she said.

He held the phone in the crook of his neck and turned the pages.

"The personals?"

"Third column, second ad from the bottom," his mother said.

He found it and read:

Financially secure man—unhappily married, late 40s, good-looking, well-read world traveler. Athletic, into golf and swimming, likes cozy restaurants and comedies, seeks young woman, late 20s–30s, attractive, affectionate, sensual, size 4 or 6, for mutually beneficial relationship.

"So?" he said.

"It's your father," his mother said.

"Mom, the guy says he's in his late forties."

"Believe me, Stuart."

"I don't think so, Mom."

"Who else would specify women by their dress size?"

"There are a million guys in the rag trade who would. Besides, since when is Dad a world traveler?"

"World War Two, darling."

"He doesn't swim."

"But he loves to sit by the pool and look at the girls."

"It's a long shot, Mom."

"I know him, Stuart. It's not."

"Well, even if it is him, so what?" he asked.

"I want you to find out."

"Mom . . ."

"I have to know."

He sighed. "So why can't you find out yourself?"

"I can't send a reply with the home phone number. He'll recognize it immediately. You have those new business numbers. He might not recognize them."

"Mom, this is ridiculous."

"All you have to do is send a reply with one of your numbers. If he answers it, you'll tell me."

"Forget it, Mom. I'm not writing a reply."

"Copy this down, Stuart."

"What?"

"Just get a piece of paper and a pen," his mother said.

When he had, she dictated to him: "Dear Sir, I am answering your ad in *New York* magazine. I am thirty-three and recently divorced with no children. I am blond, a size six and pretty. I'm told I'm sexy, although I'm not the kind of person who wears low-cut blouses and tight clothes. Since my divorce, I'm really not interested in getting married again. I love swimming and I'd like to meet a nice, tender man who is also strong and self-assured and knows his wines."

"Jesus Christ, Mom."

7

"Sign it 'Tiffany,'" his mother said.

"And what if it is him? What do I do then?"

"You answer the phone. He'll pause because he'll be surprised a man has answered. Then he'll ask for Tiffany. You hang up and call me."

"And then what?"

"And then I'll know."

2

————

THE Institute for Infant Learning, Claire's all-day pro-
gram, was six blocks away. Stuart and Laurie had
made the decision to enroll her after a traumatic experience with Betty, their Jamaican nanny.

Two months into Laurie's three-month maternity leave
she'd begun to interview housekeepers. Betty was the youn-
gest woman she'd interviewed and had the least experience.
She had no green card and was vague about her legal status
in the United States. But she and Claire had hit it off immediately, and despite some reservations, Laurie decided to
hire her at the going rate of $275 a week.

They soon discovered that Betty was temperamental and
unreliable. At least once a month she would call at eight
A.M. to say that she could not come in that day. It was
usually too late to find another baby-sitter and Stuart and
Laurie would argue over who would stay home with Claire.
Betty also liked to hang out with her nanny pals. Thus
Claire spent most of her first winter in the Kentucky Fried
Chicken on Seventy-second Street. It got so that if Laurie
wanted to find them, she called the number of the pay

phone in the restaurant. But despite these annoyances, they kept Betty because she seemed genuinely to care for their daughter.

One Wednesday in April, a year and a half later, Betty suddenly announced that she had been hired away by another family at $350 a week. Friday, she said, would be her last day. Laurie and Stuart were stunned. They had believed that Betty loved Claire, and they had come to regard her as a somewhat permanent member of the family. Furthermore, they were appalled that Betty would give them only two days' notice. Was that any way to treat people who'd given employment to an apparent illegal alien? People who paid in cash, who gave their trust, old clothes and free access to their refrigerator? Stuart and Laurie briefly discussed trying to match the other family's offer. But $350 a week was a ridiculous sum. It increased the cost of raising Claire to $18,200 a year in *after-tax dollars!* Not including Pampers.

Wounded, they had interviewed briefly for another nanny, but found them all asking in broken English for $300 to $325 a week. For that kind of money Laurie felt that Claire should at least learn to speak English without a Caribbean accent, and so they started to look at day-care centers. The Institute for Infant Learning had a low teacher-to-child ratio and a gym. It also cost about the same as college, except it was for twelve months instead of nine and you didn't have to pay for textbooks.

"Some of our recent graduates have been accepted at Brearley, Dalton and Riverdale," the director told them the morning Stuart scribbled out a check for the deposit plus one month's tuition.

Later Stuart and Laurie walked to the subway, carrying their briefcases. "We could rent a studio apartment for what we're paying a month," Stuart said.

"It's worth it," Laurie replied.

"And what did she mean by 'accepted'?" Stuart asked. "Accepted into what?"

"Kindergarten, I think," Laurie said.

10

"She has to *apply* to kindergarten?"

"It's worse than that," Laurie said. "She has to take a test called an ERB."

Stuart stopped at the newsstand and bought *The Wall Street Journal*. "She isn't even out of diapers and she's already on the fast track to Yale."

"Don't worry," Laurie said. "She doesn't have to start interviewing until she's four."

"Great," Stuart smirked.

At the end of his first day working at home, Stuart picked up Claire at IFIL. Laurie usually did not return from the office until seven, and besides, part of the reason Stuart had left his job in investment banking was to help share the burden of child care. Back home he fed her dinner. For the last month Claire had refused all foods except cold chicken, cucumber, Cheerios and vast quantities of milk. They supplemented her diet with liquid vitamins and French fries from Burger King.

At 7:25, while he sat on the living room couch reading Claire a book called *I'll Teach My Dog 100 Words,* the locks on the front door opened and Laurie came in. She dropped her briefcase, stepped out of her heels, walked directly to the couch and slumped down next to them.

"God, what a day," she groaned.

"Things busy in pillowland?" Stuart asked. Laurie was a senior vice-president in charge of marketing at Sleepwell International, the world's largest pillow producer.

"I was in meetings from nine thirty to six thirty," Laurie said.

"Business is soft?"

Laurie looked at him and rolled her eyes.

"Mommy, Mommy." Claire climbed into her lap, dragging the book with her. "Read book. Read."

Laurie glanced wearily at Stuart and then looked down at Claire. "Not now, hon, I have zero energy."

Despite her enrollment at IFIL, Claire did not yet com-

11

prehend such mathematical nuances, nor the consequences of long hard days at the office. "Read book. Read book," she insisted, pushing the book at her mother.

"No, hon, not now."

Claire knew how to deal with rejection. She began to hit Laurie with the book.

"Stop it, Claire, right now!" Laurie shouted.

Claire started to wail. Laurie let out a big sigh and looked at Stuart again, but they both knew there was nothing he could do. When Claire wanted her mommy, Daddy was not an acceptable substitute. Laurie gave in and picked up the book. Claire immediately stopped crying and settled victoriously into her mother's lap to hear the same story Daddy had already read to her three times since dinner.

Laurie read: "The first three words I'll teach my pup are . . ."

"Dig uh hole an fill ut up," Claire said. Stuart and Laurie looked at each other and beamed. It still seemed like a miracle that they had produced such an irresistably cute, passionately spoiled, brilliant, towheaded bundle of joy.

"Is there anything for dinner?" Laurie yelled later from the kitchen. Claire had finally gotten tired of the book and had settled into the couch to watch a tape of *Sesame Street* segments Stuart had recorded on the VCR. He sat next to her, reading the *Times*.

"I didn't see anything," Stuart yelled back.

"Should we order out?" Laurie asked.

It was a rhetorical question, what with energy levels hovering around zero and nothing defrosted. The real question came next: "Chinese or pizza?"

"Which is faster?" Stuart asked. It was closing in on 7:30 and he was starved.

"The Chinese kids deliver on bikes."

"Then let's have Chinese."

"What's the number?"

"Look on the phone. It's in the memory." Stuart had installed the new phones himself. The kitchen phone had ten memorized numbers. In order:

1. Doctor
2. Police
3. Fire
4. Poison Control
5. Hunan
6. Szechwan
7. Pizza
8. Video Connection
9. Super
10. Day Care

"What do you want?" Laurie asked.

"The regular."

"I forget whether that's beef with broccoli or chicken with cashews."

"So do I."

"Well?"

"Chicken with cashews."

"Cold sesame noodles?"

"Sure."

On the couch next to him Claire shrieked with fear and threw her hands over her eyes.

"What's wrong?" Laurie called from the kitchen.

Stuart looked up at the television. "Mr. Snuffleupagus."

"Fraid. Fraid," Claire cried, peaking at the furry elephantine Muppet from between her fingers.

Stuart picked up the remote and valiantly fast-forwarded Mr. Snuffleupagus into oblivion.

Dave Stroud, Stuart's friend and mentor since college, had advised him to write off everything he could against his new financial management company. But Stuart was cautious. He knew the IRS probably couldn't prove he hadn't entertained a client on nineteen dollars' worth of Chinese food that night, but until his company was firmly established he thought he better be conservative. So he paid for the meal with cash. Laurie put Claire in her high chair with a bowl of rice and they began to eat dinner.

"How was you first day at home?" Laurie asked as she mixed a little pool of Chinese mustard and duck sauce on her plate.

"I was on the phone all day," Stuart said. "It wasn't very different from being at the firm. There were just fewer interruptions and no meetings to attend."

"Then you're happy," Laurie said.

"So far."

"Did the air-conditioning man come?"

"Yes. We can either do the bedrooms or the living room, but not both. And I can't do my office at all."

Laurie stopped mixing. "Why not?"

"The wiring," Stuart said. "Apparently these prewar buildings can't handle the demand. He said we should probably put the air conditioners in the bedrooms and a ceiling fan in the living room."

"But what about your office?" Laurie asked. "It's got all that glass. You're going to broil in there."

"He said I can't run an air conditioner and the computers at the same time."

"Can't we get new wiring?"

"I asked him about that. He said people do it, but it costs a fortune."

"Well, you can't sit in there and bake."

"Bake, bake, bakerman," Claire said.

Stuart and Laurie smiled.

"I'll come up with something," Stuart said.

His fortune said, "Establish long-term goals to overcome short-term obstacles."

He stared at the slip of pink paper. "Who writes these things, MBAs?"

"Listen to this," Laurie said. " 'You will be asked to take on extra work. Do not complain. With it will come rewards.' That's weird, Peter put me on a special project with Martha today. As if I don't already have enough to do."

"Martha my dear, you have always been my inspiration," Stuart sang.

"I don't trust her," Laurie said. "She says catty things behind my back."

"Behind everyone's back, I thought," Stuart said as he peeled the orange that came with dinner.

"That's true."

"Then you can't take it personally."

"I can when it's about me."

"She's just bitter," he said. "An unmarried woman in her late thirties having an affair with a married man in the new products division. I wonder if they do a lot of pillow talk."

Laurie rolled her eyes. In the seven years they'd been together it had become a reflex reaction to his bad puns.

"That reminds me," Laurie said. "The sales conference is going to be in Portugal this year."

"Why does Martha's affair remind you of the sales conference?"

"Because that's where it started."

"In Portugal?"

"No, at a sales conference."

"I suppose this is common knowledge," Stuart said.

"You'd be amazed how many people know."

"Everyone except the married man's wife."

Laurie shrugged. Evidence of the darker side of human nature never seemed to disturb her as much as it did him. Stuart sometimes wondered what had happened in her life that made her so detached. He would probably never know. That was one of the problems of marrying late, if you could call the early thirties late. She had told him the details of her earlier life—graduated from Skidmore and Wharton, the career moves that had resulted in her becoming a VP at Sleepwell. He knew, or thought he knew, the history of her relationships since school, including the assistant district attorney she'd lived with from the age of twenty-three to

15

twenty-five. She had, she said, slept with fourteen men in her life and had told him about the significant ones. But still, her teens and early to mid-twenties were a mystery to him. What had she been like? Had she ever had an affair with a married man? Could *that* be why the thought of the poor innocent wife didn't stir up indignation in her blood the way it did in his?

"His wife works at Y & R," Laurie said. "The word is she sleeps around too."

"Probably to get back at him," Stuart said.

"Why couldn't he be getting back at her?" Laurie asked.

Stuart reconsidered. "You're right," he said. The subject of infidelity made him uncomfortable. Or possibly it was the way he and Laurie dealt with it that bothered him. He picked up his chopsticks.

"Don't you feel sometimes like we've been brainwashed?" he asked. "I mean, we fit all the yuppie stereotypes. Young upwardly mobile New Yorkers with a child living on the West Side. We put our daughter in Ivy League prep day care. We discuss infidelity like it was just some bug going around. Like the flu. Why do I feel like I'd rather die than let anyone catch me eating Chinese food in New York with a fork?"

"Stuart, if you want to eat it with a fork, go right ahead and I won't tell anyone."

"No way."

"Why not?" Laurie asked.

Stuart grinned. "It wouldn't taste the same."

3

———

E VERY night at 8:30 Claire insisted on dancing. Stuart
tuned in a rock station on the stereo and he and
Laurie took turns accompanying Claire while she
spun on her knees, rocked on her back and hopped up and
down in a neonatal version of break dancing. At 8:45 Stuart
changed her into an ultra-absorbent Pamper and put her in
her pajamas. Claire asked for a bottle of milk and lay down
on her favorite spot on the living room couch. Five minutes
later she was asleep.

Stuart carried her into her room and placed her in the
crib. She looked up at him sleepily and waved, opening and
closing her little hand. "Bye bye, Daddy."

Stuart kissed the tip of his finger and touched her cheek.
"Bye bye, baby."

He found Laurie in the kitchen, bending into the refrigerator, picking at the leftover sesame noodles. She had
changed out of her office clothes and into a short white
terry-cloth robe she'd lifted from the Boulders Rockresort
after last year's sales conference. Moving behind her, Stuart

placed his hands on her hips, pressed his groin against her buttocks, and did a soft grind.

"Careful," she said.

"Of what?"

"You'll knock me into the cottage cheese."

He slid his hands up her waist. "Claire's asleep."

"In her crib?"

"Uh-huh." He slipped a hand inside the robe.

"Stuart . . ."

"I'm in the mood for luuuvvve . . ." he crooned.

She straightened up and faced him. "And I'm exhausted," she said.

He sat in bed naked, reading an article in *Parents* magazine about schoolchildren and AIDS in which sex was described as "exchanging bodily fluids." It sounded like something Martians did. On the other side of the bedroom Laurie slipped out of her robe and threw it on a chair. Then she undid her bra and took off her gold necklace and Rolex. She always slept in her panties.

She got into bed and opened the latest issue of *Manhattan, inc.*

"Peter asked me what you were doing now," she said. "He said he'd like to invest some money with you."

"I don't know. I'd feel funny if I lost your boss's money."

"Stuart, when have you ever lost anyone's money?"

"I've been incredibly lucky. Getting out of the market three days before Black Monday . . ."

Laurie shook her head and looked in the magazine.

"You told him the minimum investment?" Stuart asked.

Laurie nodded.

"And he'd hand it over just like that?"

"If you're so nervous about investing other people's money, why did you leave the firm?"

"Because that's all I did there. Other people's money. OPM. Sounds like opium. It is opium."

18

Laurie leaned over and kissed him on the cheek. "You'll do fine. I have confidence in you."

She turned back to her magazine. The funny thing was, she really did have confidence in him. And so did everyone who invested with him. Most of what he did was just plain work—reading quarterly reports, crunching numbers, talking to company managements—but he also had a knack, especially when it came to hedges in the options market. At Bingham Brothers, his former employer, he'd predicted the 1987 Crash and saved them a ton of money.

Next to him, Laurie absentmindedly reached under her panties to scratch herself. Stuart wondered if he should suggest sex again. Early in his banking career, he and Dave Stroud had once had an argument over which was more satisfying, having sex or making money. Stroud had argued that despite the immediate pleasures of sex, making money resulted in longer-term and more tangible rewards. But to Stuart it had been no contest. Sex won every time. Now, ten years later, he wasn't so certain. Whether sex or money won usually depended on which he'd generated less of the previous week.

He glanced again at Laurie. After she'd had Claire, her body had changed. Her breasts had sagged just a bit and her tummy bunched up when she sat. Several times he'd found her naked, sideways to the mirror, with tears in her eyes. He told her it didn't matter, but it was an issue in which his opinion did not count. Instead she'd started going to a gym at lunch and, with the aid of low-impact aerobics and a high-fiber diet, had made her body return to its pre-Claire shape. If anything, he thought she was even more attractive now than before she'd had Claire, attractive enough so that he was certain—even though she denied it—that men in her office had to be interested in exchanging bodily fluids with her.

"My mother called today," he said.

"What did she want?" Laurie answered without looking up from her magazine.

"She says my father is running ads for single women in *New York* magazine."

"He probably is."

Stuart stared at her. "What makes you say that?"

"Oh, come on, Stuart, you know he's a letch."

"My father? I thought you liked him."

"I do, but that doesn't mean he can't be a letch."

"What makes him a letch?"

Laurie looked up. "Well, for one thing, every time we go out to dinner with him and your mother he stares at all the young women. And no matter what we talk about, he always seems to find a sexual nuance in it."

Stuart thought about arguing that point, then decided against it. He was more interested in sexual nuances himself at the moment.

Laurie had told him a thousand times that creating the right mood was important, but where did you start when you were both sitting in bed, reading? Best not to sneak around. He turned off his reading light and slid toward her, kissing her bare shoulder.

"Hi, Woof," he said softly, sliding one finger gently down the slope of her breast. In moments of affection they called each other "Woof," "Woofer," and "Woofee." After seven years together he could not recall now how these names had started, or what they were supposed to mean. But sometimes in company, especially after a few drinks, they would accidentally use one of these intimate forms. Friends pretended not to notice.

Laurie gently removed his fingers from her breast. "I'm sorry, hon. I'm just too tired."

"You sure?"

"Maybe tomorrow night."

"You could just lie there while I ravage you," he said. "I mean, you don't have to be energetic."

"Not tonight, Woof. I'm a mother, a businesswoman and a wife. I just don't have the energy to be a lover, too."

20

★　　★　　★

He was uncertain as to what form her fatigue took. She said she was tired, and yet she stayed up and read for nearly an hour. Still, he did not begrudge her. Their sex life was basically sound, if somewhat less frequent since the arrival of Claire. Sometimes lately, he opened his eyes in the midst of exchanging bodily fluids with her and discovered that she was scratching her nose or biting at a cuticle. But then he too was not nearly as passionate as he had been in the early years of their relationship. Things had changed markedly after Claire's birth, but he'd read enough issues of *Parents* to feel comfortable that this was the case with a majority of his fellow Americans.

Just before midnight the blare of sirens rushed in through the open bedroom window. They sounded close.

"You think it could be us?" Stuart asked.

"I don't smell any smoke."

"Could be upstairs," he said, getting out of bed. He walked toward the front of the apartment and went into his office without turning on the lights. Through the thin gauze curtains on the French doors, he could see flashing red and white beams. He pulled the curtains back. Three fire engines were in the street, and firemen were jogging into the Excelsior Arms carrying oxygen tanks and fire axes, their open raincoats flapping. Only a couple of room lights were on in the hotel and Stuart could see the silhouettes of several anxious residents peering out of their windows, but most of their neighbors appeared to sleep through the sirens and noise.

A few minutes later the firemen dragged their equipment back out, talking and laughing among themselves. It was a false alarm. Stuart got the feeling that the firemen and most of the hotel's residents were used to them.

He was just about to return to bed when a light went on in the woman's room on the ninth floor. A second later *she* leaned in the open window, a black silhouette backlit by

21

yellow light. Stuart stood by the French doors, doubting she could see him in his darkened office. To be safe, he pulled the curtain closed until there was just a slit to watch through.

He could not see her face, just her dark outline. This time she was dressed. The image of her leaning on the window sill reminded him of prostitutes in Europe—but who tried to attract men from nine stories up? As he watched, she rose from the window and retreated into the room. A moment later the light went out. His first thought was to return to bed, but something made him stay. He waited a minute, then two. Then the glass doors in front of the hotel opened and she came out dressed in a light, frilly white blouse, tight dark slacks and high-heeled pumps. She was going out. At midnight.

4

"MOMMY, Daddy, uppee, uppee." The little cry came from the nursery. Stuart opened one eye. The clock said 6:26.

"Mommy, Daddy, uppee, uppee. Uppee!"

Laurie shifted next to him. "Your turn."

"I got up yesterday morning," he said.

"I did," Laurie mumbled.

"Mommee! Daddee! Uppee! Uppee!"

"You did not, I did."

"Then I got up last night."

"No one got up last night."

"*Mommmeee! Dadddeee! Upppeee!*"

"Please, Stuart."

Hell, he was up anyway.

Claire was standing in the crib, wearing her yellow Big Bird pajamas and rattling the wooden bars with her hands. "Muck, muck, muck."

"Come here, pumpkin." He picked her up. Just lately she

had started putting her little arms around his neck when he lifted her. That simple gesture alone made life worthwhile.

He carried her to the kitchen and took a baby bottle of milk out of the fridge. She grabbed it eagerly and then squirmed to be put down—a freestanding drinker.

"Let's go to Daddy's office," he said.

She followed him down the hall, holding her bottle to her lips with one hand and dragging a stuffed brown puppy in the other. He had not seen her pick up the toy. It had appeared in her hand as if by magic. She seemed to have stuffed animals secreted all over the apartment, always within reach.

"Phone, phone," she said, automatically associating Daddy's office with his primary activity. He imagined that if she could speak more clearly and someone asked her what her father did for a living, she would say, "He makes phone calls."

In the office she pointed at the VDTs. "Tee, Tee. Occar, Occar."

"No, babe, these aren't televisions. You can't watch *Sesame Street* on them."

Claire's baby brow furrowed and then she nodded. "Occar all gone, all gone."

She played by the French doors while he spoke to England. It was always best to call before seven in the morning New York time and get the English brokers before lunch. After lunch the phone calls seemed to take twice as long.

"Cah, cah. Pane, pane." Claire had parted the curtains and was identifying various modes of transportation visible from the window. Meanwhile a broker in London told Stuart a joke: ". . . so the bloody horse lets out a terrific fart. Of course the princess is absolutely mortified. She turns to the sheikh and says, 'I'm dreadfully sorry.' To which the sheikh replies, 'Quite all right, dear. I thought it was the horse.'"

The broker laughed. Stuart laughed. Claire turned from the window and said, "Funny, funny."

The phone call ended. Stuart got up and stood behind Claire at the windows.

"Take a taki, take a taki," Claire said.

A cab had pulled up in front of the Excelsior Arms.

"Pretty lady." It was *her,* in the same clothes she'd gone out in at midnight. Where was she coming from? Work? Play? He looked at his watch: 7:03.

He got Claire into her school clothes and fed her a dropperful of vitamins. Laurie had showered and was in the bedroom.

"You want to take her or pick her up?" Stuart asked as Laurie put on a gray silk dress.

"I'll take her if I have time," Laurie said. "I've got a nine-o'clock meeting with Peter and I can't be late." She straightened the dress and put on a string of pearls. "What do you think?"

"Looks good."

"Read book, read book," Claire said.

"Okay." He took Claire out to the living room and sat down with her on the couch.

Two pages into Richard Scarry's *Color Book* Laurie emerged from the bedroom. She was now wearing a red dress with the pearls. "How's this?"

"It's fine."

"Are you just saying that or do you really mean it?"

"I think you look fine," he said. "I thought the gray dress looked fine too."

"It didn't."

"Well, this does."

Laurie went back into the bedroom. Stuart continued to read to Claire. The clock in the VCR said 8:15. They were getting late.

A few minutes later Laurie was back, wearing the gray dress again. "How's this?"

"I thought you didn't like that dress," Stuart said.

"I changed the shoes," Laurie said.

Stuart looked at her shoes. They were black. "Well, okay, that looks good. Now you better get going or you're going to be late."

"I'll be ready in a second," Laurie said. She went back into the bedroom.

They finished the Richard Scarry book. Stuart looked up at the clock. It was now 8:25. "Hey, Laurie?"

She came out again. Now she was wearing a black dress. "What do you think?"

"I think that the most important thing about this meeting is what you contribute to it, not what you wear."

Laurie shook her head. "You're so wrong, Stuart. How I look has everything to do with how I am perceived and thus how I perform."

"This is not a liberated businesswoman I hear talking," Stuart said.

"This is a realistic businesswoman you hear talking," Laurie said. "Now tell me honestly if you like it."

"I honestly liked the gray and red dresses better."

Laurie looked at the clock. "Great. Now you've made me late."

"How have *I* made you late?"

"You said you don't like this dress, so I'll have to change."

"But I said I liked the gray and the red ones and you changed them anyway," Stuart said.

"Well *I* didn't like them," Laurie said and went back into the bedroom.

Stuart decided that the only way Laurie was going to get dressed was if he got out of there. He picked up Claire, placed her in the stroller and rolled her to the door.

"I'll take Claire," he called. "See you later." And before Laurie could ask him to judge another outfit, he was out the door.

Stuart usually sang songs to Claire as he pushed her to IFIL. "Row, Row, Row Your Boat" and "The Bus Song" were two of her favorites. He enjoyed it. He could stroll

26

along and sing and no one would think he was a nut. Had he tried it without Claire he would have been deemed certifiable.

At the entrance to IFIL they encountered heavy stroller traffic. Things often got backed up around 8:45 as parents rushed to drop their kids off and run to the office, often to discover as they left that they had a crying child clinging to their cuffs.

Almost all the adults who brought their children to the center were working parents like Stuart and Laurie. Stuart had a nodding acquaintance with a few of them, but knew them only as Melissa's mother or Howie's father. The people who ran the center seemed competent and sincerely interested in children. To Stuart's and Laurie's relief, Claire had taken to the place almost immediately and seemed eager to go each morning. After an initial period of guilt about sending her there, Stuart now felt pretty good about it. He assumed Laurie did, too.

There were twelve kids in Claire's room, divided up among a head teacher and two assistants. In almost every other room at the center the teachers were women, but in Claire's, two were men—the head teacher, Sam, and one of the assistants, Eddie. Stuart didn't mind Eddie, who was a pleasant young effeminate man who hennaed his hair a deep auburn color. But Sam was definitely disconcerting. He was about six-foot-two, must have weighed 220, shaved his head to baldness and wore a thick Fu Manchu mustache. He usually wore an old white T-shirt and faded jeans and had large tattoos of dragons on his arms. To Stuart he looked like one of those gay leather freaks who hung around the S & M bars in the West Village engaging in all sorts of deviant sexual behavior. But after speaking to several other parents, Stuart had been reassured that beneath the unorthodox exterior lurked a gentle and devoted caretaker.

Once inside the center Stuart folded the stroller and hung it on a bar with the other strollers. Claire ran ahead to her room and stood in the doorway looking in at the kids sit-

27

ting at a low table making a mess with their morning breakfasts of graham crackers, peanut butter and juice.

"Uppee, uppee." She reached up toward Stuart. It was her habit to get cold feet for a second before the school day began.

Stuart lifted her into his arms and carried her into the room.

"Issa, Issa." Claire pointed at a little girl named Melissa. Then, "Cracka, cracka," for the grahams and "Butta, butta," for the peanut butter.

Sam was standing at the sink, pouring apple juice from a yellow pitcher into a baby bottle. Stuart noticed that he'd added a second gold hoop to his right earlobe. "So how's my Claire today?" Sam asked, putting the pitcher down and reaching toward her.

"She's fine," Stuart said. Claire let go of him and reached toward the tattooed teacher. A second later she was in Sam's arms. Stuart felt a lump in his throat. God only knew what those arms had held last night.

Sam kissed her on the cheek. "Want a cracker, little one?"

Claire nodded and the teacher gave her a graham. Stuart started to back away.

"Uh, Stuart," Sam said.

He stopped.

"There's been some diarrhea in the three's class," the teacher said. "Arnie and Jessica went home with it yesterday. Claire hasn't had any, has she?"

"She's been pretty firm," Stuart said, feeling a little awkward. He wasn't sure whether it was talking about his daughter's feces that made him feel funny, or just the fact that he knew the answer.

"Well, I want you to keep an eye on it," Sam said.

"I definitely will," Stuart said.

Claire waved at him, opening and closing her hand. "Bye bye, Daddy."

"Bye, babe." Stuart left the room, closing the door behind him. A few weeks ago he had been an investment banker at a top-tier firm, earning a six-figure salary. Today he was being told to watch his daughter's feces by a day-care teacher who was probably lucky to make three hundred dollars a week. He reminded himself that leaving the firm was a choice he'd made voluntarily. It was just going to take some getting used to.

5

"DECAPUTATION insurance," the young man on the ladder in the middle of the room said.

"I'm sorry?" Stuart said, patting his forehead with his handkerchief.

"I says I'll install a ceiling fan for ya but ya better get decaputation insurance."

Stuart guessed the man was about twenty-one. He was wearing paint-spattered jeans and a red bandanna around his forehead. He was standing on the top step of a short metal ladder, having just driven a nail into the ceiling and pulled it out. He seemed annoyed.

"You mean you can't guarantee that the fan will stay in the ceiling?" Stuart asked.

"Look, all yous got up here is concrete an' ash," the young man said, getting down off the ladder. "You show me a beam, 'cause I can't find it. Dat's the trouble with dese old buildings."

"Well, I don't want to have my head chopped off," Stuart said.

"Right." The man snapped his ladder closed and headed

for the door. Stuart followed, feeling badly that he'd wasted the man's time.

"Thanks," Stuart said.

"For what?" the man asked and left.

He went back to his office, wondering. How did people in these buildings cool themselves? Servants with large feather fans?

The phone tweeted. He switched on the speaker. "Hello?"

"You sound like you're in Giants Stadium." It was Eliot Berger, one of his closest friends within his local calling area.

"It's my speakerphone."

"Can you get off it?"

"Why did I get it if no one will talk to me on it?" Stuart asked.

"Maybe you should ask yourself that question," Eliot said. "Now how about it? My life is falling apart and I don't like the idea that the whole world can hear."

Stuart picked up the receiver. "What's wrong?"

"Wait, let me go back to my seat," Eliot said.

He heard the faint sound of talking and laughter. A few seconds later Eliot got back on.

"Where are you?" Stuart asked.

"Somewhere over Buffalo."

"Where're you going?"

"Denver for an afternoon meeting. Then San Francisco tomorrow. Phoenix the next day. Then Houston and Palm Beach. Get some tennis in on Saturday and fly home in time for the party. If I still have a wife."

"What are you talking about?"

"Something you can't repeat to anyone. Not even Laurie."

Stuart's second line started to flash. "I have to put you on hold," he said, switching lines. A friend of his father's was on 0801, a dentist who had recently invested $200,000 with

31

him. Stuart said he'd call back in a minute and switched to Eliot.

"Okay."

"I think Carol is having an affair."

Stuart turned to his desk-top calendar. On a page with three consecutive years printed on it, he circled the date with a red pen.

"I think it's with someone she works with," Eliot said. "I may have even met the son of a bitch once."

"You're two months early," Stuart said.

"What?"

"For the last three years you've called me on an average of once every eight months to say you thought Carol was having an affair," Stuart said. "The last time was six months ago."

"This time I'm serious," Eliot said.

"Last time you were serious too."

"Listen to me, douche bag. I mean it. She's just not there for me lately. She's been working late a lot. Some Saturdays. There have been a couple of overnight trips. I get home from out of town and she acts like I'm a stranger."

"You probably are at this point."

"Look, what am I supposed to do? I can't make deals sitting in my office. You know that."

"Let's not have that discussion again," Stuart said. "And anyway, it sounds like she's just busy. Laurie has the same schedule."

"No, it's more than that," Eliot said. "She's been busy before, but this is different. She even goes into the office *early* sometimes. This is a woman who I used to have to drag out of bed in the morning."

Now 0802 flashed. Stuart put Eliot, somewhere over Buffalo, on hold again, then took care of the other call.

"Okay, I'm back."

"And, uh, things have been kind of slow in bed," Eliot said.

"Mind if I ask for how long?"

"Well, actually, it's sort of gotten gradually worse ever since we got married."

"Maybe you should read *Parents* magazine," Stuart said.

"What? Why?"

"They have articles on things like that. You discover that the majority of your contemporaries are going through the same thing. It may not help your sex life, but at least you'll feel better."

"That's what you do now that you're working at home? Read *Parents* magazine?"

"Don't be condescending. I squeeze it in between *Barron's* and *The Wall Street Journal*. It helps put life in perspective."

Again 0802 flashed. "Hold on." Stuart switched, dispatched, returned.

"You think I'm imagining this thing with Carol?" Eliot asked.

"I don't know, but from what you've told me, it doesn't sound like enough to convict."

"She didn't say anything to Laurie last weekend, did she?" Eliot and Carol had joined them for dinner at the Albuquerque Barbeque, the latest step in the mesquitization of Manhattan.

"Not that Laurie told me about. But I don't imagine Carol would talk about it even if it was true."

"You're probably right." Eliot seemed pacified. "So anyway, the apartment looks great. I should be congratulating you, not griping. How do you like working out of the house?"

"Considering I've been doing it for exactly five days I better withhold an opinion."

"Too quiet?"

"No, the phone still rings just as much."

"You put a lock on the refrigerator yet?"

"Don't have to. There's never anything to eat in it anyway."

"That would be my downfall. So look, maybe you ought to forget what I said about Carol. Just talking to you makes

33

me see how dumb it is. It's probably just my overactive imagination. You got a baby-sitter for Saturday night?"

"Roger. What's the agenda?"

"Nothing fancy. Just four couples and dinner."

"And the ETA?"

"Seven thirty. Not later than eight."

"See you then."

Later, Dave Stroud called. Dave had been Stuart's freshman advisor at Penn. After graduation he'd gone to Stamford Business and then to the private investment house of Bingham Brothers, a low-profile firm widely recognized by the investment world as one of the best. Now at thirty-eight, Dave headed the mergers and acquisitions group, had about twenty-five bankers reporting to him, and had once made a million dollars a year.

"What's long and hard and every Polish girl gets one on her wedding night?" Dave asked.

"I don't know."

"A new name."

Stuart chuckled. "That's actually funny. Where'd it come from?"

"Lazard Freres."

"I would have guessed Solomon."

"So how's the Miller Fund?" Dave asked. "Made your fortune yet?"

"Ha, ha."

Dave cleared his throat. "Now seriously, the trading desk is a mess. Jamison came in this morning before the market opened and told me the last offer he made you. Has anyone told you you're out of your mind?"

"What good is it if you have no life outside work?" Stuart said.

"Can I be frank?" Dave asked.

"You always are."

"You were amazingly lucky. But it can't last. In a few

more years you'd have made partner. Then you'd have a life. No one expects partners to put in eighty-hour weeks."

"When was the last time you put in less?"

"I do it because I want to."

"I'm not sure I believe that."

"I do."

"Well, I want to watch my kid grow."

"Is it fun?" Dave asked facetiously.

The image of Sam ordering him to watch Claire's feces popped into Stuart's mind. "Yes, I happen to be enjoying it. Every day Claire learns new words. It's really great."

"I have news for you," Dave said. "She's going to learn to talk whether you're there or not."

"That's not the point."

Dave cleared his throat again. "It's a good thing Jamison doesn't remember that I'm the one who said you'd do so well for us."

"I saved the firm millions. And you always were a lousy judge of character." After college, Stuart had worked as an analyst for two years. Then he'd gone to Columbia B-school and had joined Bear, Stearns after graduation. He'd stayed two years, started to earn a reputation as a trader, and then asked Dave if he could come to Bingham. That had been five years ago.

"Now listen," Dave said. "Seriously for a moment. Jamison wanted to know what it would take to bring you back."

"Forget it."

"Just make something up—so I can tell him I tried."

"Well, less travel for one thing."

"That's nothing."

"Okay, let's see. I'd want total autonomy."

"Still not good enough."

"How about a bigger performance bonus?"

"Those days are over, Stu."

"Well, then, what the hell. Tell him I want profit sharing."

"Short of partnership, of course."

"*Just* short of partnership."

"Good," Dave said. "Now this is getting interesting. What else?"

"Jesus, I don't know."

"What about salary?"

"Okay, half a mil guaranteed."

"Great. You just hit the Twilight Zone."

"Whew."

Dave laughed. "Had you worried there, huh?"

"You're telling me," Stuart said. "For a second I thought I might have to come back."

A telephone rang in the background. "I have to put you on hold," Dave said.

The phone became quiet. In the distance Stuart could hear two faint voices talking on another line. He frowned. Maybe he *was* insane to give it all up.

Dave got back on. "Have to run. Quick, what's the story with this party Saturday night?"

"It's just four couples. Eliot and Carol always make it nice."

"She's the knockout and he's the banker over at Fast and Easy who wants a job here?"

"Right."

"Maybe he can have your old job," Dave said.

"He'd love it," Stuart said. Eliot had been trying to ingratiate himself with Dave for years.

"Wasn't he going to send over his résumé?" Dave asked.

"He didn't?" Stuart was surprised.

"I never got anything. Anyway, is he any good?"

"You and he are my closest friends," Stuart said.

"So? I asked if he was any good."

"To be honest, I don't know. He must be doing all right because four months ago they forked over seven fifty for a one-bedroom penthouse on Riverside."

"For a *one-bedroom*?"

"Phenomenal view."

"Of what? New Jersey?"

"That's the way he wants to spend his money," Stuart said. "Ask him about it on Saturday night."

"Sure," Dave said. "And how about lunch one of these days?"

"Can you come up here?" Stuart asked.

"For lunch? Are you serious? I wouldn't even have time to shake hands."

"Then how about meeting halfway?"

"Uh, sure. Listen, I really have to return that other call. I'll see you Saturday night."

"Okay." Stuart hung up and looked around the hot, cramped room that was his office. His terminals were stacked on his desk, along with keyboards, telephone and calculators. A small mountain of quarterly reports lay on the floor next to a pile of spreadsheets. A Steinberg print hung on the wall. It occurred to him that he'd recreated the same damn office he'd had at Bingham. The only difference was, it was a long way from Wall Street.

6

His social life had evolved into dinners out on Saturday nights and sixteen phone calls a week with friends and family. His business life consisted of about thirty-five phone calls a day. And he didn't have anyone to go to lunch with.

When he wasn't on the phone he sometimes had a fantasy in which he wrote a big check to Laurie's account and then just disappeared for a while. It was not that he didn't love her, he did. And he was crazy about Claire.

But there was an overpowering sameness about his life and work. Even having Claire, moving to the new apartment, and going on his own didn't change it. It was the same damn office, same damn job. He made money for himself and for others, but he rarely saw the fruits of his labor. On his computer he could graph the financial portfolios of his clients. But when he turned the terminals off, there was nothing. He wasn't so much bothered by the fact that making money the way he did had little socially redeeming value as he was by the fact that it no longer excited him. The research was boring, even the amounts of money he handled weren't interesting. They were nothing compared to the huge institutional accounts he'd handled at Bingham.

"What are you doing, Woof?"

Laurie startled him. It was early evening and he was standing at the French doors in his office with the lights out, peeking through the part in the curtains. Across the street someone was in the hotel room with *her*. Another woman. Taller, with short blond hair. They were both moving around. Dressing and primping for a night out, he guessed.

"Just checking the temperature," he said, turning away from the window and pulling his J. Press tie a little tighter. Laurie stood in the doorway, backlit. She was wearing a red silk dress and the gold necklace he'd given her for her birthday.

"You look nice," she said, blocking his exit.

"So do you."

"Kissee, Woofee," she said, imitating Claire's habit of adding "ee" to words.

He kissed her, and inhaled the perfume she saved for special occasions. Her lips tasted sweet. It was amazing how changed she was on Saturday evenings after a day spent decompressing from the office. "You smell good," he said.

She parted her lips slightly and pressed her body toward him, sliding her hand down over his zipper. "Did you ever notice that the more we dress up, the more it makes us want to undress?" she asked in a low voice. The baby-sitter was in the living room with Claire.

"We could be late," he said, aware that this particular mood was becoming more and more elusive in their lives.

"I'd rather leave early," she said. "Besides, Eliot will be frantic if we're not there before Dave and Joan."

"I guess. I just hate to miss an opportunity."

She squeezed him gently. "It should still be here when we get back."

She turned and headed toward the living room. He

reached into his pants pocket, realigned himself so as not to startle the baby-sitter, and then followed.

He often thought that the greatest areas of speculation in the city were not in real estate and securities, but in trying to figure out who was gay and what his friends' salaries were. As his generation slid into their mid-thirties, less attention was paid to where they'd grown up and how much they'd inherited (unless it was a truly spectacular amount). Attention now focused on what sex you preferred, what you earned and how you spent it.

Among his friends, no one spent money more exotically than Eliot and Carol, the proud owners of the one-bedroom penthouse on Riverside with a view of New Jersey. They had Baccarat crystal, fresh-cut flowers daily and a Jasper Johns print on the wall. They thought nothing of taking a two-thousand-dollar weekend in Bermuda, or paying four hundred dollars for a pair of tickets to a charity ball. Yet Carol worked as a copywriter on the in-house advertising staff of a company in Westchester. It was a job that could not pay much. Stuart could only surmise that Eliot had somehow survived the plunge.

Carol met them at the door. She was a great-looking, shapely blonde, the sort of woman Stuart would have sworn only existed on television and in men's magazines. Tonight she was wearing black slacks and a cream-colored translucent blouse. She and Laurie and Stuart exchanged kisses and compliments on how wonderful they each looked. Stuart noticed that he could almost see through Carol's blouse and sheer brassiere underneath. It took all of his willpower to keep from staring.

"Thank God you're here," Carol said. "Eliot was beginning to panic."

"He shouldn't have," Stuart said. "Dave and Joan are always late."

"Well, go reassure him," Carol said.

Stuart left Laurie with Carol and walked through the din-

40

ing alcove where a young woman wearing black slacks and a white shirt was setting out hors d'oeuvres. Eliot was at the bar unit in the living room. He was wearing a Paul Stuart blazer and gray slacks, a blue shirt, a Hermès bow tie and what Stuart had always called silk suspenders but were currently called braces. Eliot's were red with white ducks stitched in them.

"Hey, there he is," Eliot said. "One G and T coming up." He unscrewed a small Schweppes tonic. "Dave isn't pissed at you for leaving Bingham, is he? I mean, there won't be any friction between you two tonight, right?"

"What do you think?"

"I don't know, man. I figure you guys are good friends. But you did leave the place."

Stuart shrugged.

Eliot handed him his drink. "You think he's got any openings in mergers and acquisitions?"

"If he does, bankers'll kill for it. But go ahead and send him your résumé."

"Yeah, I know. I've been meaning to." Eliot took out a martini pitcher and poured half a bottle of Tanqueray in. "Think he'll be impressed?"

"Dave?"

"No, my great uncle."

"With what?"

Eliot waved his hand toward the large, semicircular window looking out over the Hudson and New Jersey. The lights of Fort Lee and the George Washington Bridge shimmered in the dark. "With this. The best view on the West Side. A five-hundred-dollar catered dinner served care of the Columbia bartending service at twelve an hour plus car fare."

"I don't know. Dave doesn't impress easily."

"What do you think he pulls down? Half a mil?"

"Couldn't tell you."

Eliot smiled. "But you could guess. I bet you'd come within twenty-five grand of every partner at Bingham."

41

Stuart sipped his gin and tonic. "Playing much tennis?"

"No, too much time on the road. I try to book an hour with a pro whenever I have a free afternoon, but usually all I have time to do is check out and head for the airport."

"What's all the traveling about?"

"Road shows. Sell dinners. Hand jobs for the institutional guys."

"New issues?"

"New issues, refinancing, convertible bonds, the works. Hey, did you hear about the Polish newlyweds?"

"The one about what's long and hard?" Stuart asked.

"No, that was last week," Eliot said. "This week they get into bed on their wedding night and he says 'Fuck you.' Then she says, 'Fuck you.' Then he says, 'Fuck you.' Then she says 'Fuck you.' Then he says 'Fuck you.' Then she says, 'Fuck you.' Then he says, 'Fuck you.' Then she says, 'You know, this oral sex is pretty boring.'"

Stuart groaned.

The doorbell rang. It was still too early for Dave and Joan. The young woman from the Columbia bartending service answered the door and two men came in. One appeared to be in his late forties, his gray hair cropped close to his head, a thick salt-and-pepper mustache and a gold hoop through one ear. He was wearing a black linen suit with something lavender and collarless underneath. His associate was considerably younger, with teased blond hair piled on top of his head, but the sides shaved closely. He was wearing a billowing pink blouse and black Spandex tights, a sort of fay swashbuckler with a trace of mascara and rouge on his cheeks.

Eliot grinned at Stuart. "Come on, I'll introduce you."

Stuart followed him across the room. "This is Edward and Sean."

They shook hands. Edward said hello. Sean said delighted. Someone was wearing perfume.

"Edward gave Carol her first job in New York," Eliot said.

"Where?" Stuart asked.

"A nightclub called Space, if I recall correctly," Edward said.

"Edward's a designer," Eliot said.

"I put her on a moonscape wearing a bikini and sitting under a beach umbrella," Edward said.

"That was how I first met her," Eliot said. "I saw her in that bikini and thought, 'This is it.'"

"He waited until I was on my break," Carol said, coming out of the kitchen. "And then he asked me if I'd take a shower with him." She kissed Edward and Sean hello.

"What did you say?" Sean asked.

"No," said Carol.

"So I came back the next night and asked if she'd prefer a bath," Eliot said. "And she said yes."

"Oh, bullshit," Carol said. "He came to the club for a week and finally I said I'd have a drink with him, but only if my friend could come too. What did I know? It was my third week in New York and I was just a country girl from Ohio."

"I knew I had to nail her fast." Eliot slipped his arm around her waist. "Before she was taken."

"I think Edward and Sean need drinks," Carol said, moving away.

Eliot slapped his hands together. "Okay, boys what'll it be?"

"Scotch on the rocks," said Edward.

"A white wine for me," said Sean.

Eliot turned to Carol. "And for you, my dear?"

"Dramamine." She went back into the kitchen.

Dave and Joan arrived, were introduced to Edward and Sean, and immediately donned plastic smiles. Stuart knew Dave would be amused by the company, but Joan, a tall, big-boned ultra-WASP, would not. She suffered no fool lightly, nor chose to deviate from any norm. He watched as she appraised the situation with near-panic in her eyes. The least he could do was save her.

"Good to see you again, Joan."

"Oh, Stuart." She looked immensely relieved.

"Get you a drink?"

"Yes. White wine, please."

He fetched her a glass and returned. Joan and Dave had lived in the city briefly after college, in a brownstone in the West Seventies. One Friday evening two men had followed Joan into her building. One had held a knife to her throat while the other removed her jewelry and purse, causing her such fright that her bladder gave out and ruined a new pair of four-hundred-dollar leather boots. Later that night she made Dave drive her to her parents' house in Oyster Bay, where she persuaded them to lend Dave and her the down payment for a house. Two years passed before Dave could convince her to return to the city to see a show.

"When are you and Laurie going to come out for a sail?" she asked.

"Laurie gets seasick."

"Have you tried the patch behind the ear?"

"Last summer. She slept for eighteen hours."

Joan nodded and glanced over at Sean, who was having an animated conversation with Laurie. Eliot and Edward were standing near the window, considering the view. It seemed to Stuart that Joan couldn't wait to leave. She turned back to him.

"And how is Claire?"

"Great. We're really happy with the place she's at."

Joan scowled. "The place?"

"We've got her in a day-care center."

"I see."

It was obvious to Stuart that she didn't. "It's called the Institute for Infant Learning. For a small fortune they give her breakfast and lunch, bring in special music and art teachers every week, and give us monthly reports on her gross motor coordination."

"You mean it's not one of these state-run facilities that's always getting in trouble for child abuse."

"No, of course not."

"How nice."

Their conversation limped along. Stuart had been told he was a good listener. But the trouble with listening was the remarkable diversity of boring subjects you had to pretend to be interested in in order to be deemed a worthy and likable soul. He felt badly for Joan (they could hear Dave in the kitchen, talking and laughing with Carol) and tried to think of subjects she'd been interested in the last time they'd spoken. It was like playing host to a foreigner. How could he have so little in common with someone who only lived twenty-five miles away?

"You race, don't you?" he asked.

"Oh, yes, we took a third in our class for preseason." Joan brightened, then proceeded to treat him to twenty minutes on racing a J-35, followed by ten minutes on North Shore real estate, five on the wonders of microwave convection ovens, and an encore on quarry tile. All the while Laurie was across the room with Sean, smiling, jabbering, aglow.

A few minutes later, Stuart excused himself and followed Laurie into the bedroom where she'd gone to telephone the baby-sitter. He found her sitting on the bed, receiver at her ear.

"Everything okay?" he asked after she hung up.

"Claire's having a bottle and watching TV. I told Jane to have her in bed by ten." She got up and looked at herself in the mirror.

"Having a good time?" he asked.

"Not bad."

"You looked like you were enjoying yourself."

"That Sean is a character. Ask me anything about head lice."

"Serious?"

She nodded. "He works at a fancy nursery school on the

45

East Side. Believe it or not, even rich kids get head lice. How did you do with Joan?"

"She spent five minutes telling me why we must get a microwave convection oven."

"But we have one," Laurie said.

"I know. But she was so earnest. I didn't have the heart to tell her."

Laurie gave him a sympathetic look. "Maybe we can slip out after dessert, Woof." She kissed him and headed back toward the living room.

Stuart ducked into the bathroom and put his drink on the edge of the sink. Someone had made serious use of the toilet and then neglected to flush. He was glad he discovered it and not Joan. He flushed it away without much ado, taking pride in his mature treatment of the situation. After changing Claire's diapers innumerable times, plus dealing with some out-of-diaper experiences, it would take a bit more than an unflushed toilet to unsettle him.

When he came out, Carol was sitting on the edge of the bed, lighting a cigarette.

"You know why cigarettes are dangerous?" Stuart asked.

She shook her head and exhaled a cloud of smoke. "I don't care."

"They travel in packs," Stuart said.

Carol smiled. "I should have known you wouldn't lecture me." Holding her cigarette in the corner of her mouth, she reached inside her blouse and adjusted her brassiere.

"I've been trying my best not to stare," Stuart said, staring.

"Go ahead, everyone else does."

"Something wrong?"

She shook her head. "Nothing."

"Why don't I believe you?"

She shrugged and tugged at her bra strap again.

"You don't wear that blouse to work, do you?" he asked.

"Forget it. It's hard enough to get men to take you seriously when you're a woman. I don't need them leering at me all day."

Perhaps he could cheer her up. "You know, I've never had that problem," he said, sitting down next to her on the bed. "Maybe someone should come up with a line of brassieres designed to make breasts appear smaller so women at work won't get leered at. You could call it the Executive Bust Decreaser. Maybe the name of the company would be Boobs R'nt Us."

"You're drunk, Stu."

It occurred to him that she might be right. It was nearly nine and he'd had two and a half strong gin and tonics and no dinner. He glanced at her blouse again. This talk about the female anatomy was starting to have an effect on him. To speak college Freudian, his normally ironclad superego was springing id leaks. In fact, he suddenly felt the most incredible urge to reach over and feel her up. As if it were an adjunct to the conversation. A sort of show and tell and feel. As if Carol would understand because she knew men had been wanting to do that all her life. And he was a man. Albeit a married man. A family man.

Carol slipped her hands behind her, arching her back slightly. She took the cigarette out of her mouth and looked for something to tap the ash into. Stuart offered his half-finished drink.

"Go ahead. You're right, I've probably had too many already," he said.

Carol tapped her ash in. It made a hiss. She looked gloomy. Stuart decided to try a different tack. "Is it a problem at work?"

"No, not really," Carol said. "But I wish I could get into a New York agency. Working in an in-house agency is so Mickey Mouse."

"Sending your résumé around?" Stuart asked.

"With samples of what?" Carol asked. "Catalogue copy and publicity releases? That's trained-monkey work."

Stuart now regretted that he'd brought up the subject. It only seemed to worsen her mood.

Carol took a deep drag on her cigarette and sighed smoke. "I'm sorry, Stu. I shouldn't complain to you. You're a guest and this is supposed to be a party."

It was rare to see her so sad and vulnerable. The libidinal urge Stuart had just succeeded in forcing down bubbled up again, and for a moment in his somewhat inebriated state he was madly, impossibly in love with her. He wanted to shelter and protect her, take her away to a deserted tropical island and make love to her nonstop for seventy-two hours. *Do you realize,* he asked himself, *that for as long as you remain faithful to Laurie you will never, ever again have the opportunity to taste another woman's lips? Or touch her breasts? Except, possibly, to administer cardiopulminary resuscitation?*

Carol suddenly stood up and faced the large wall mirror, pushing her fingers through her hair. "So how's the kid?"

A wave of shame swept through him. She must have sensed it, he thought, feeling angry with himself. "Uh, you mean Claire? She's great. I recommend them highly."

"What? For me?"

"For anyone." He watched her in the mirror, still feeling the tug of his libido. Damn it, he and Laurie should have acted on their urges first and *then* come to the party. At least he wouldn't be sitting there feeling like a sixth-grader with a hard-on for the new substitute teacher.

"We're not ready for that," Carol said. "We'll never be ready for that."

"Why not?"

"It's, I don't know, so grown up."

"So are you."

"Aw, shucks, I'm just a little kid. Didn't you know?"

"Carol, I honestly never knew a little girl who looked like you."

She glanced back at him and smiled like a little kid. Again he felt it. God, the impulse was strong. But luckily, or unfortunately, depending on how you looked at it, it was

48

nothing more than an impulse. This was Carol, Eliot's wife. And Eliot was already overly paranoid about her. And short of murder and rape, Stuart could think of absolutely nothing more wrong than putting the moves on a good friend's wife.

"Putting the moves on my wife, huh?" Eliot said, coming into the bedroom at that moment. He seemed to have built-in radar when it came to Carol.

"Doggone, you caught us," Stuart said with a grin.

Eliot put his arm around Carol's waist. His movements were clumsy, due no doubt to his affection for very dry martinis. "With a woman this beautiful, I can't let her out of my sight for a second."

"You're telling me," Carol said.

Dinner reminded Stuart of a job interview he'd had shortly after college at a large women's wear company whose CEO was a friend of his father's. Stuart had had no intention of working there, but he went because his father had gone out of his way to set it up. The man who interviewed him was a senior vice-president. It was immediately obvious to Stuart that the VP was not only taking time from an extremely pressing schedule, but had no idea what kind of jobs were available there for young men fresh out of college. In fact, the man began the interview by explaining, very apologetically, that as far as he knew, it was a company policy not to hire people unless they had previous work experience in the field. Stuart was tempted to leap from his seat, shout, "Wonderful!" and leave. But he didn't. Just as the VP was no doubt conducting the interview as a favor to the CEO, Stuart stayed as a favor to his father. The interview lasted for almost an hour with the VP monotonously reciting the job ladder for each of the company's five divisions. Stuart pretended to be fascinated. Finally, the VP finished and asked what area Stuart thought he might be interested in. Stuart thought about it for a moment and said, "Actually,

I'd like to get a job on Wall Street." The VP smiled, then stood up and shook Stuart's hand. "So would I," he said.

At dinner, it was Sean who valiantly rose to the chore of keeping the conversation going, telling sadly humorous stories about being a gay teenager growing up at West Point, the son of a military science professor.

But by the time dessert was served, even he had run out of stories. No one else seemed to know what to say, so Eliot, who'd switched from martinis to wine, tried a joke about a Norse god endowed with a truly Olympian member who visits a very mortal and drunken prostitute.

"After they finished, the whore says, 'Who are you anyway?' And the god says, 'I'm Thor.' So the whore says, 'You're thor? I'm tho thor I can hardly pith.'"

The silence was broken by a ringing telephone. A moment later the Columbia student came out of the kitchen and asked if a Joan Stroud was there. Joan went to the phone, but returned quickly.

"It's the baby-sitter," she said. "Brent isn't feeling well. I'm afraid we'll have to go."

Dave and Joan departed, followed a short time later by Edward and Sean. Eliot, Carol, Laurie and Stuart sat around the dinner table, finishing their coffee, and watching the candles drip.

Eliot slouched in his chair, his bow tie undone and his sleeves rolled up. He smirked. "Great party."

"I had a good time," Laurie said. "And dinner was delicious."

"I enjoyed myself," Stuart said.

"You can't blame yourself because her son wasn't feeling well," Carol said.

Eliot gazed at them and grinned. "Either I'm drunker than I think, or the three of you are the biggest bullshitters around."

Early in their relationship, Laurie had debunked the myth of having an orgasm every time they made love, making it clear that there would be occasions when she was happy to accommodate him while she herself had no desire to be satisfied. At those times she made herself an active, panting participant—aside from occasionally scratching her nose or biting a cuticle—and accomplished her chore in workmanlike fashion, skillfully and quickly. Stuart had his pleasure, but always felt a little guilty that he had not given her hers. He confessed this to her once and she laughed, telling him he'd been brainwashed by the 1970s.

Then there were the nights when Laurie was in the mood. "Tease me," she whispered that night. They were lying in bed, under a light quilt. The newly installed air conditioner was humming softly. Laurie rolled onto her stomach, her face turned away from him. He proceeded gingerly and with the hands of a surgeon. It was tricky. Over the years, the right mood had become a fragile and elusive entity, easily destroyed by the wrong move, the baby's cry, even the neighbors' fighting. Gentleness and surprise were the keys to success. She did not like to be touched in the obvious places at the obvious times. Propped up on his elbow beside her, Stuart had to be both sensitive and inventive, monitoring her progress and at the same time coaxing it along. To go too slow would risk losing it. Go too fast and he might snap her out of the mood. It was a nerve-racking, tiring process and in the midst of it he sometimes imagined that he was on the bomb squad, handling a live one. Except instead of defusing it, his job was to make it explode.

Afterward, they lay entwined in the dark.

"I feel badly for Carol," Laurie said.

"Why?"

"Because Eliot is so . . . I don't know. Anyone else would have known it wouldn't work."

Stuart thought it over. "I guess he thought he was proving something to Dave about his worldliness."

"Why?"

"Who knows? Eliot has crazy ideas. Maybe he thinks

51

Dave needs someone to handle gay mergers and acquisitions."

Laurie rolled over and looked at him in the dark. "I hate to say this, Woof, but I really don't understand what you see in him. He's so showy and shallow."

"Look at it from his point of view," Stuart said. "He's a graduate of Hofstra trying to compete in a world dominated by Harvard and Yale. You have to admire him for even trying."

"Is that admiration or pity?"

Stuart didn't have a ready answer. He realized that he had just given Laurie the same justifications for his friendship with Eliot that he always gave himself. But it wasn't the complete truth. A guy needed a friend he didn't have to feel competitive with. Someone he could relax with, someone whose relative position was clearly defined. Eliot had been a presence in his life since B-school, a breath of fresh laissez-faire who'd caustically ridiculed Stuart in class for his idealistic schoolboy talk about a career in the public sector. Stuart knew he was right. They could sit around talking about monetary theory and fiscal reform, but basically they were going into business to make a buck.

He'd liked Eliot for his lack of pretensions, his camaraderie and general high spirits. After graduation they'd moved to a one-bedroom apartment on East Fifty-fourth Street together. From there they had hit the Street, working, drinking and chasing women until they dropped from exhaustion, slept like dead men and then started all over again.

When Eliot married Carol, Stuart had been his best man. A year later Stuart married Laurie. Their lives changed. Settling down seemed to be synonymous with becoming serious. Up till then they'd clawed their way up in the financial world together, but Stuart, with his low-key gamesmanship and push-button charm, fit in, while Eliot, with his faux pas and rough-edged aggressiveness, didn't. Stuart blossomed at Bingham Brothers. Eliot could do no better than an enormous investment firm with outlets in department stores and shopping malls all around the country. That had been the beginning of a certain amount of strain between them.

Stuart kissed Laurie on the cheek and then rolled onto his back. He slipped his hands under his head and looked up through the dark. "It's one of those things that just keeps going. After a while you stop wondering why."

Laurie moved toward him and he realized she wanted to be held. She snuggled tightly into his arms, and felt warm and smooth.

"Just lately I've begun to think that that's the way it is with everything," she said wistfully. "I mean, we just keep going and try not to wonder why. Sometimes I think it's incredible that this is all there is to life. I mean, that there isn't more. You have a husband, a child and a job. You go out, see your friends and go on vacation. Year after year it's the same."

Stuart knew what she was talking about. "I wonder if it's that way everywhere or just New York," he said. They had gone through a period of writing away to chambers of commerce. They had spoken to real-estate agents in Connecticut, Westchester, Long Island, Boston, Atlanta and San Francisco. In the end they had moved exactly twenty-two blocks.

Laurie propped herself up on her elbow. He could just make out her outline in the dark. "When we were looking at other places to go, I realized that I've been in New York so long I'm afraid to leave. I'm not sure I could deal with life somewhere else."

"It would probably be easier," Stuart said.

"I know," Laurie replied. "That's what scares me."

7

———

SHE had a regular routine—rising around three or four in the afternoon, taking a shower, staying in her room until the evening and then going out for the night. On sunny afternoons she would plant her hands on the windowsill and arch her back, face up toward the summer sun like a lioness. Only she had a black mane, and shapely breasts that jutted out into the sunlight.

He watched her and wondered how she could be so unconsciously uninhibited. Surely she had to be aware that someone, either down on the street, or in the buildings across from her, could see. Why didn't it bother her? Why *did* it bother him?

The phone tweeted. He went to his desk to pick it up.

"Stu?" It was Eliot.

"Hmm?" He walked back toward the French doors, stretching out his newly purchased extra-long phone cord.

"I fucked up, right?"

"Well, I'm not sure that it helped."

"Christ, I'm an asshole."

"Hmm." Across the street she left the window for a moment, then returned cradling a black telephone receiver against her ear. She stood in the sunlight, her lips moving rapidly, the fingers of her free hand skipping up and down the tight coil of the cord. She had breasts like a teenager's. He could not stop looking at them.

"Stu, you there?"

"Oh, uh, yeah." He forced himself to turn away.

"Do you really think it was a mistake inviting them?"

"I don't know, Eliot. Joan didn't seem too keen on the idea."

"But everybody in New York knows a couple of fags." Stuart coughed.

"All this New York sophistication is bullshit," Eliot said. "We all try to be so cool, so with it. But look where we came from. Nice middle-class families in the suburbs. The spooks and fags are okay as long as they don't move next door, right? And I was dumb enough to think it had changed. Dave probably thinks I'm a jerk."

"I think Dave tries to see the brighter side of things," Stuart said.

"Then I still have a shot?"

"I have no idea, Eliot. And I don't understand why you won't send him your résumé and go in for an interview. He's a good guy. Even if there's no opening he'll still talk to you."

"Yeah, I guess. I just feel like it's who you know in this business that counts."

"But you already know him."

"Yeah, you're right. Shit, man, I can't believe how grim this has all gotten. Remember when we first started? Making our fifty grand a year, partying all the time, chasing every woman we saw. Then everything got so fucking serious. All you have to do is blow one deal and it'll cost you a whole year's bonus."

"It's all part of the game."

"If I'd wanted games I would've been a tennis pro," Eliot

55

said. "I could stand around all day tapping balls to kids and rich housewives."

"You'd be tan," Stuart said.

"I'd be broke."

"Maybe you're right, Eliot. Maybe you do take it too seriously."

"Look who's talking. A guy who quits his job at the best firm in the city because he feels like he wastes too much time in meetings. You feel good now, but try telling me it's a game the next time Black Monday comes around and you've got fifty investors bringing suit against you."

Stuart chuckled. "Hopefully when that happens I'll go short again."

She was also on the phone a lot. Sometimes, while she spoke, she paced quickly from the window into the shadows of the room and back, like a kite weaving rhythmically in the wind. He began to assimilate her patterns of movement. Each time she disappeared from sight he knew he only had to wait a few moments until she returned.

One afternoon there was a young man in the room with her. Stuart had guessed that she was in her mid-twenties, but if this boy was any indication, then she was even younger. The boy was blond. He was standing near the window, pulling a shirt over his hairless chest. Stuart guessed that he couldn't have been older than eighteen. *She* remained naked, moving quickly around the room. She always moved quickly. The boy slowly buttoned his shirt, his head turning to follow her as she scampered back and forth. Then he disappeared from sight, possibly, Stuart thought, to use the bathroom.

As soon as he had gone, *she* went to the window and stuck her ass out into the sunlight. She put one hand on each cheek and spread them. Stuart couldn't figure out what in the world she was doing. Then it came to him. She wanted to pass air in a small room without being discovered. Across the street he laughed out loud.

56

8

THE phone tweeted; 0804 lit up. Stuart stared at it for several rings before picking it up.

"Uh . . . Is there a young woman named Tiffany there?"

It was his father.

"Hello? Is anyone there?"

"Dad, it's Stuart."

Pause. "Stuart? What? How?"

"It's a strange story, Dad."

"I don't understand."

"A couple of weeks ago Mom asked me to answer a personal ad in *New York* magazine. She insisted it was you. I guess she was right."

"I can't believe this," his father said.

"You're not the only one."

"How could she know?"

"I think the part about the sizes gave it away."

"Oh . . . why?"

"Most people who run ads in the personals don't specify the dress size of the person they want to hear from."

"Well, what did she want you to do?"

"She wanted me to tell her if you called."

"Will you?"

Stuart sighed. "No."

"Well, I appreciate that. That bitch."

"Dad . . ."

"Well, it's true, Stuart."

"I'm sure she's not too happy with you either."

"Well, it's a goddamn crime that she's dragged you into it."

"She must feel like she needs an ally."

"Why can't she stand up and fight on her own?"

"You're a tough character, Dad."

"Damn straight I am."

Stuart stood up and carried the receiver to the French doors. It was becoming a habit. Only it was eleven A.M. and *she* wouldn't be up yet.

"So, uh, how's Laurie and my little granddaughter?"

"They're fine, Dad. You wouldn't want to tell me why you ran a personal ad in *New York,* would you?"

On the fifth floor of the Excelsior Arms, a young man was leaning on his elbows out of one of the windows. He was bare-chested and had a large blue tattoo on his left arm near the shoulder. In his right hand he held what appeared to be a black ashtray. A green window shade had been pulled down behind his head to his back, and his shoulders were pulsating as if someone was steadily thumping him from behind. He picked up a half-smoked cigarette from the ashtray and puffed on it.

"Life is complicated, Stuart."

"I've heard," he said. The young man continued to pulse and puff. The rhythm was unmistakable.

"Your mother and I have not seen eye to eye for years."

The young man took a last deep drag and crushed the cigarette into the ashtray. He looked bored.

"I've worked hard all my life and I deserve some respect," his father said. "It's become obvious that your mother has no interest in providing it."

"But Jesus, Dad, *New York* magazine?"

"You think I should have tried the *Voice*? Your mother doesn't read that."

"That's not what I meant."

Across the street the young man stopped pulsing. Like a turtle disappearing into his shell he slid backward and vanished behind the green window shade.

"When you get to be my age, you realize that you only go through this life once," his father was saying. "And how limited your time is. It makes no sense to be unhappy."

"Maybe you two should separate for a while."

"Well, I've thought about it, but I can't. She couldn't survive without me. She can't take care of herself."

"She runs her own travel agency and she can't take care of herself?"

"You wouldn't believe the things I have to do."

"Like what?"

"I can't tell you, Stuart. It's not for your ears. She's just a very, very difficult woman."

Almost simultaneously 0801 and 0803 flashed on. "Gotta go, Dad."

"You won't tell her I called?"

"I said I wouldn't."

"You're a good son."

That evening he picked up Claire at IFIL. He found her curled in Sam's arms, sucking her thumb.

"Eric had it today," Sam said as he handed Claire over.

"Had what?" Stuart asked, only half paying attention. Claire put her arms around his neck and puckered her little lips for a kiss.

"The diarrhea," Sam said gravely. "I had to send him home."

59

It was no longer just plain diarrhea. It was now The Diarrhea. Like The Plague.

"Is there anything we can do to stop it?" Stuart asked.

Sam shook his head. "They'll just have to get through it."

On a scale between minor bumps and bruises and major diseases like chicken pox and measles, Stuart wondered where The Diarrhea fit in. Just to be safe, he took Claire home via Broadway, stopping at the Love Store to pick up an extra box of Pampers. He felt a slight twinge of embarrassment as he pulled a fifty-cent coupon from his wallet and slid it over the counter to the cashier. It was confusing for his self-image. In the matter of an hour he had gone from managing more than ten million dollars in investments to coupon clipping. Actually, the coupon had come in the mail. He didn't even have to cut it out. It was stupid not to use it. He wouldn't throw two quarters in the garbage, why throw out a coupon?

He hooked the cardboard handle of the Pampers box over the handle of the stroller. As he turned away from the counter, a strikingly attractive young woman waiting in line behind him smiled. She was strawberry blond with a model's chiseled looks, wearing a skintight royal blue Spandex aerobics suit, pink leg warmers and white sneakers. He could have sworn he'd seen her in a commercial sipping a diet soft drink or using an antiperspirant. Had she seen him use the coupon? Or was she smiling because it was cute to see a daddy pushing his little curly-haired daughter in a stroller?

Stuart smiled back and pushed the stroller out the door. Women like that never smiled at him when he was alone. In fact, strolling on the sidewalks lately, he'd played a little game, sending out meaningful glances at women in their early twenties, just to see what their response would be. The results were discouraging. To be honest, the young woman in Spandex wouldn't have given him a second glance if it hadn't been for Claire. Oh, perhaps if he'd been wearing one of his nicer suits, she might have. But, in a way, that was another telling development. Working out of his home he had no reason to wear a suit, and yet it was one of the hardest habits to break. He'd become so accustomed to the message an expensive-looking dark-olive gaberdine sent out, not only to business associates, but to women, cab drivers, practically everyone, that out of a suit he felt, well . . . unemployed.

Halfway home, a slim dark-haired woman wearing a blue Laura Ashley print dress and white Reeboks glanced into the stroller and then smiled at him. Stuart's return smile was small and pinched. Did they think that he was safe and harmless because he had a kid? Did pushing a stroller some-how neuter a man in a woman's eyes? Maybe he could rent Claire out to single men. They could push her around town and every time an attractive woman smiled, they could explain that they were only the uncle. It would probably beat running personals.

Back in the apartment he gave Claire a bottle of apple juice and set her up in front of the TV with *Sesame Street*. Then he went into the bathroom and stood in front of the mirror. He was thirty-four and the hair in the front of his head was beginning to thin. Depending on how he combed it, you could see clear through to the scalp in some places. He had been aware of it for years, but only recently had others begun to notice. People sometimes stared at his hair-line when they spoke to him.

His body and face had also changed. He was the same weight he'd been in college and yet his waist size was two inches larger. It was harder to quantify the change in his face. His features, he felt, had become thicker, his eyes a bit more deep-set. Regularly, he used a tweezer to pull short black hairs from the tip of his nose and longer ones out of his ears.

It was as if through his twenties he had been unaware that he was growing older and now was suddenly faced with it. And it wasn't just the changes in his body. In his twenties he had slept like a rock, but now he would wake some nights at four A.M., his mind full of possible investment plays, and lie there for an hour or two before he could sleep again. He was also beginning to recognize his foibles—always telling himself it was time to cut out desserts and start exercising, going out of his way to avoid confrontations, seeking an emotional equilibrium that avoided both highs and lows. He spent more and more time in front of the television, and when he watched sports he found himself rooting for the veteran players and being particularly intolerant of the younger stars who messed up their lives with cocaine.

The hands of the clock could not be turned back or stopped, and God knew he had plenty to be thankful for, but this abrupt and unequivocal evidence that he was growing older frightened him. The previous February, for the first time in his life, he'd stopped at a newsstand and purchased the *Sports Illustrated* swimsuit issue. Recalling what his mother had said about his father looking at girls in bathing suits made him cringe. This can't be happening, he told himself.

9

H E found himself spending more and more time at the French doors. In the mornings, while *she* slept, there were others to watch. The young man with the tattoo had a steady lover, a tall, skinny, balding man with a thick mustache. He seemed to stay for several days at a time, and when he did, they made love almost continually, usually with the shades up.

Stuart found himself not repulsed, but fascinated. They engaged in what he understood to be the highest-risk forms of sex and yet appeared to take no precautions against AIDS. The balding man with the mustache always did it to the young man with the tattoo, and often in positions Stuart had never dreamed of. They would arrange pillows and furniture to facilitate their activities and then the balding man would rub some Vaseline Intensive Care lotion (Stuart recognized the bottle) onto himself and go to work, often for five or ten minutes at a time. Then he would stop, rearrange the younger man beneath or beside or in front of him and begin again, pumping steadily for what seemed like an eternity until he either came or stopped and changed positions.

Sometimes it seemed to go on for hours. Sometimes they both smoked while they did it.

They must know, Stuart thought. *Can it be they don't care?* In the early afternoon he would start waiting for *her* to appear. There were a few days when he was disappointed, when the room remained dark until it was time for him to leave to pick up Claire. On at least two occasions, he saw young bare-chested men in the room. Sometimes he saw the tall blond woman with the crew cut, but once there was a bare-breasted black woman and on another occasion there were two additional women in the room, trying on and taking off clothes.

It was summer and there was no air conditioning in the hotel, but Stuart could not imagine that heat alone caused them to spend so much time in the nude. He began to wonder what they were doing in there. As he stared at endless columns of glowing yellow numbers on the dark-green computer screen, his mind would wander. He imagined the inside of her room draped with colored fabrics and pillows. Shafts of bright sunlight streamed in through the windows onto luxuriating young naked bodies. He didn't imagine orgies. They were *beyond* orgies. Sometimes Stuart pictured himself in the room, being accepted despite his thinning hair and thickening middle. He imagined coupling with sleek, willowy olive-skinned women in languid, unhurried heat. Women who *knew* he was married . . . but didn't care.

One afternoon after lunch he discovered her standing on a chair by her windowsill, her body in full view, clad only in a pair of black bikini briefs. She was reaching upward, toward the top of the window frame, apparently hammering something. With each swing of the hammer, her breasts rose and bounced. Stuart stood by the French doors, hidden behind the curtains, transfixed—until the phone tweeted.

"I have to talk to you." It was Eliot.

"Hello, Eliot, how are you?"

"Christ, you sound cheerful."

"I can't help it. I am standing here watching a lovely naked woman across the street literally in full view from head to toe."

Eliot groaned. "I wish you hadn't said that, Stu. It's gotten intolerable."

"What has?"

"With Carol. It's been over a month. I can't even ask anymore. I just can't stand listening to her excuses."

"Maybe you both should go see someone."

"You want to know how bad it is?" Eliot said, going on as if he hadn't heard the suggestion. "This morning I got turned on by Tropic Anna."

"What?"

"You know, Tropic Anna. I was having grapefruit juice and she began to look good."

"I didn't know she had a name."

"Yeah, it's on her hat. She's at least a nine. Maybe a ten. And talk about grapefruits. I kept turning the container so I wouldn't have to look at her, but she was on three panels."

"Eliot, are you making a joke or is this serious?"

"I'm making a joke because it's so serious I don't know what the hell else to do. *This is the fucking end of my marriage!*"

He had never heard Eliot talk like that. He turned away from the French doors and sat down at his desk.

"First of all, where are you?"

"Why the hell does that matter?" Eliot asked.

"It matters. I have to be able to imagine you."

"I'm in the St. Louis Airport, okay? I'm at a pay phone across from the imitation MG-TD body that fits any Ford, VW or Chevy chassis. Jesus Christ, why should it matter where I am? I'm never in one place long enough anyway."

"Okay, now tell me what's going on."

"I just told you, dipshit."

"If you continue to be abusive, I'm going to hang up," Stuart said.

"Okay, I'm sorry," Eliot said.

"What does she say?"

"Mostly she says she doesn't want to talk about it. I kept her up half the night trying to make her talk about it and the only thing I got out of her was that she doesn't know what's going on either. Meanwhile, I touch her and she is like ice. The icewoman who never cometh."

"Eliot, you have to go talk to someone."

"I'm talking to *you*."

"I mean both of you. With a professional."

"She won't."

"Have you asked her?"

"About two hundred times."

"Oh."

"There has to be someone else," Eliot said.

"When does she have the time?"

"Are you kidding? I'm out of town at least four days a week. When *doesn't* she have time? If it's a guy at work they could be humping at some motel during lunch. If he's in the city he could be over practically every night."

"Hmm."

"Listen, Stu, I have to find out. I'm going insane not knowing. I search her pocketbook while she's in the shower; I go through her clothes. I swear, I even check her underwear."

"Maybe you should hire a detective."

"I looked into it. Do you know what those guys cost? What if they don't see each other for a couple of weeks?"

"I'll lend you the money."

"Sure. I bet you can really afford it going into business on your own, carrying that new apartment and your kid in the day-care center of the stars."

Stuart chuckled. "It's not that rough."

"Well, spare me the charity, okay? I can always take a week off and rent a car without telling her. I'll just pretend I'm going to the Coast. She'll never know."

Stuart pressed his fingers into the corners of his eyes. "I can't believe we're talking about Carol."

"I know," Eliot said. "I keep telling myself I can't believe it either. I mean, if I find out, I'll kill her, I really will."

"Will you do me a favor?"

"What?"

"Before you do anything crazy, call me."

"Okay."

"Promise?"

"Yeah, I promise."

Stuart hung up and sat at the desk for a moment, staring at the Quotron. Each time Eliot decided that Carol was cheating on him he became so convinced that it was hard for Stuart to pass it off as mere jealous neurosis. Eliot was like a salesman who truly believed in the product and got you to believe in it too even though you'd used it six months before and hated it. But what if he was right this time? Carol was an extremely sexy, inviting woman. Any man could fall for her.

Stuart shook his head and got up. He went back to the doors to see if *she* was still at the window. Across the street he could see nothing. She'd hung a white window shade.

10

IT bothered him for the rest of the afternoon. Was he the reason she'd hung the shade? Had she noticed him lurking by the French doors like a Peeping Tom? The thought mortified him. But what about her? Wasn't she just a bit of an exhibitionist? Oh sure, she would claim it was her right to prance around her room in the nude, but come on, what did she expect?

Then again, he didn't think he'd been that obvious. Certainly, if she was aware of him, she'd never glanced in his direction or given him any kind of clue. That left the possibility that she'd simply decided on her own to put up the shade. Or that there was someone else on his side of the street who was also watching her. Someone who really was a pervert.

Later, at IFIL, Sam informed him that the march of The Diarrhea continued unrelented. Some of the staff had even come down with it. In Claire's class, only she and Melissa Messing had remained unaffected.

Stuart was secretly pleased. He thought it showed that Claire came from good diarrhea-resistant genes. An extra box of diapers, however, couldn't hurt. So he pushed her home on Broadway, pausing to get more Pampers at the Love Store, then passing record stores, card shops, laundromats and restaurants. It was early evening and he gazed in at the patrons dining near the windows of various restaurants. Outside Peligro De Mayo, a Chinese-Cuban greasy spoon that did a big business with taxi drivers, he suddenly stopped. *She* was inside, sitting sideways to the window at a small table with the woman with the blond crew cut. Their plates were filled with black beans and yellow rice.

She was talking and gesturing with her fork. Her companion smoked a cigarette and ate. Stuart was certain that the blond woman was a dyke. Even on that warm evening she was wearing a leather jacket, black jeans and boots. Up close for the first time, he saw that *her* features were harsher than he'd imagined. *Her* mouth was large, her teeth were big and slightly horsey, her nose a bit flat. Still, he thought it was an attractive face, one that he could easily imagine becoming exotic and sensual in the right circumstances.

He was so surprised to see *her* that for the moment he forgot himself and stared. Suddenly aware of him, she paused from her conversation and looked through the window. Then she looked down at Claire in the stroller and smiled. Stuart smiled back, but *she* turned away and began talking to her friend again.

"Stuart?"

He turned to find a man with curly graying hair and gold-rimmed glasses standing next to him on the sidewalk. He was wearing New Balance tennis sneakers, blue shorts and a gray Adidas T-shirt. On his chest he carried a drooling infant in a blue Snugli baby carrier. He looked vaguely familiar.

"It's Howard," the man said. "I shaved the beard off. And this is Gwendolyn." He stuck his pinky into the drooling infant's mouth and she sucked on it. It seemed unhygienic.

Stuart knew Howard from the tennis courts in Riverside Park near Columbia, where he had sometimes played during B-school. Howard had always been at the courts. Once, when Stuart asked him what he did for a living, he'd said he was writing a book. As far as Stuart could tell he'd been writing it for about ten years, and didn't seem to be in any hurry to finish. Nor did money appear to be a pressing need. In the meantime Stuart still saw him around the neighborhood, sometimes on his bike with his tennis racket.

"This is Claire," Stuart said, gesturing to his daughter, who was busy eating an apple.

Howard stooped down. "Wow, she's adorable."

Claire looked up at him, little bits of apple pulp clinging to her cheeks. "Baby," she said.

"Yes," Howard said, nodding in that exaggerated way all adults did with little kids. "A little baby. Only seven months old. And how old are you?"

Claire stared blankly at him and then turned back to her apple.

"She doesn't know about age yet," Stuart said.

Howard rose again. "Yeah, it's really hard to figure out what these kids know when. I thought by seven months Gwen would be using the Apple IIe. So how goes it? How's uh . . .?"

"Laurie."

"Right, Laurie. Stupid of me."

Stuart nodded, but not in agreement. "It goes well. What about you? I didn't know you'd gotten married."

"Well, I'm not actually. I mean, this is our kid. We just haven't officially tied any knots."

"Oh?"

"Her mother's name's Ann and she's a painter. Believe it or not we met up at the Riverside courts. She was getting off and I was coming on and that was it."

"That's a hell of a way to get pregnant," Stuart said, making a joke.

Howard smiled. "Well, it did happen a little faster than we expected. I mean, we're really glad. We probably would have gotten to this point sooner or later anyway. Hey, is that a MacLaren?"

Stuart looked down at the stroller. He'd never noticed what brand it was.

"We got an Aprica," Howard said. "I'm really sorry now. I mean, it's incredibly sturdy, but it's heavy. I hear the MacLarens are better, only they don't last as long. If you have a really active kid they kick them apart."

"Claire's fairly low-key."

"I can see. God, she's pretty. I see a lot of Laurie in her, but a lot of you too." He gestured at the box of Pampers. "Just pick 'em up at Love's?"

"Yes."

"They've got about the best prices around," Howard said. "You see those coupons that came in the mail the other day? I spent half the morning running around trying to bribe mailmen to give me their undeliverables. I mean, everyone tells you having a kid is expensive these days, but Pampers are a fortune."

Stuart recalled now that Howard had often complained about the cost of things, and had rarely brought his own tennis balls to the courts. Perhaps he wasn't as well off as Stuart had imagined. Instead of being independently wealthy, he might only be independently middle-class.

"Don't ever try those store brands," Howard said. "We did that right after Gwen was born. What a mess. They don't have any elastic around the legs and everything just drips right out. Well, you probably know that. How old did you say Claire was?"

"Two years."

"So do you have someone taking care of her? Laurie didn't seem like the type who'd stay home."

"No, she isn't. We had someone for a while, but now we have Claire in day care."

"All day?"

Stuart nodded. Howard looked surprised. Someone with less couth might have said, "She seems kind of young for that." Howard didn't have to.

"We have a woman," Howard said. "I didn't know the first thing about this stuff, but Ann . . . She stayed home with Gwen for about three months and then the next thing I knew she was down in Riverside Park everyday, scoping out the nannies, asking who was unhappy with the kid they had or felt they weren't being paid enough. And sure enough she found this great Jamaican woman who was being paid peanuts. Ann offered her more money and that was it. The woman is incredible. Maybe not the most reliable in the world, but great with Gwen."

Stuart was no longer smiling. "Just out of curiosity, what's her name?"

"Our Jamaican lady? Betty. Why, you know her?"

I don't believe it, Stuart thought.

Howard squinted at him. "Hey, you're not going to steal her from us now that I've told you how great she is, are you?"

"I wouldn't dream of it," Stuart said, clenching his jaw.

"I didn't think you really would," Howard said. "But that stuff happens all the time. People steal nannies left and right. They're a valuable commodity, and they know it. Even Betty's started to make noises. We started her with one week's paid vacation. Now she says she wants two. But I don't know how much longer we'll keep her anyway because we've been looking at houses in New Jersey. We just don't feel like this is the right place to bring up a kid. I bet you guys would disagree with that. You're dyed-in-the-wool urbanites, right?"

"We've talked about moving out, but we just bought a new place here so I guess it won't be for a while."

"I can see it. I mean if you're tied to jobs in the city."

And tied to making a living, Stuart thought, feeling hostile.

Little Gwendolyn started to cry.

"Must be titty time," Howard said. He looked down at Claire. "I guess Laurie nursed her until it was time to go back to work, huh?"

"Actually, we never quite succeeded. Claire is a formula baby."

Howard nodded gravely. "Well, gotta go. Give my best to Laurie and good luck with the little one."

"The same to you and Ann."

Howard strode off. Stuart felt like taking what was left of Claire's apple and chucking it at the back of his head. *Nannynapper! Son of a bitch!* Do you know what misery you caused us? Stuart couldn't help recalling those horrible weeks right after Betty left. How sick at heart he and Laurie had been. The sick days and vacation time they had both taken when no one could be found to watch Claire. And the interviews and tryouts with women who didn't stay for one reason or another. The uncertainty they felt each time a new woman took Claire out to the park. Stuart could remember following familiar-looking strollers into stores to make sure it wasn't Claire being kidnapped. Once he'd even chased a red Subaru station wagon two blocks to a stop light, gasping for breath and staring into the backseat while the bewildered parents rolled up their windows and locked their doors. From every angle except the front, the child in the car had looked remarkably like Claire.

Stuart gritted his teeth. Ann knew what she was doing when she stole Betty. Good luck in the suburbs, *bastards!*

73

Suddenly he remembered where he was and why. He glanced back into the window of Peligro De Mayo. *She* was looking at him, her plate now empty, her companion lighting another cigarette. Stuart felt flushed and embarrassed. *She* must have seen the anger in his face as he recalled Betty's departure. She had caught a glimpse of him he usually did not want to reveal. But then again, touché. He turned away and pushed Claire toward home.

11

LAURIE got home at 7:15 that night. Stuart was sitting on the couch reading Mother Goose stories to Claire.

"How come wolves get such a bad rap in Mother Goose?" he asked as she sat down with them.

"Maybe they deserve it," Laurie said, giving Claire a hug.

"I don't know. I thought I read once that they were the only truly monogamous animal. You think Mother Goose is subtly against monogamy?"

Laurie gave him a look that said she was too tired to deal with it. "Any ideas for dinner?"

"I haven't looked in the fridge."

"I think there's some cheddar cheese," she said. "We could have grilled cheese sandwiches or melted cheese on broccoli."

Stuart grimaced. Laurie had gotten onto a melted cheese kick lately. At least twice a week they had it on something—broccoli, baked potatoes, even tuna fish. It was that damn microwave oven. Put anything on a plate, throw a slab of cheese on top, and *poof!* you had dinner.

"I think I'll order a pizza," he said, getting up and going into the kitchen.

While they waited for the delivery, Stuart made a salad and Laurie gave Claire a bath. Wearing the dress she'd worn to work—the sleeves rolled up to her elbows—she kneeled on a bath mat beside the tub, soaping Claire down while she played in the water with some plastic cups and a *Sesame Street* bath book. Stuart finished the salad and joined them, sitting on the toilet seat with a gin and tonic.

"I ran into Howard on the street today."

"Howard?"

"The tennis player. The one I used to play with when I was at Columbia?"

"Oh, right."

"His girlfriend is the one who stole Betty from us."

Laurie looked up at him.

"Betta, Betta, all gone," Claire said.

"How do you know?" Laurie asked.

"He told me. He was bragging about how smart his girlfriend was to go down to the park and ask around about who felt they were being underpaid. I almost hit him when he said the woman they found was named Betty. Anyway, his girlfriend had a little girl. He says they're looking for a house in the suburbs."

Claire started splashing.

"Please don't, hon," Laurie said. "You'll get Mommy's clothes wet."

"Clothes, wet, wet."

"I wonder if we should have moved out of town," he said.

"Then I could leave for work before Claire woke up in the morning and get home after she'd gone to bed at night," Laurie said. "I wouldn't even know I had a child."

"You don't have to work those hours."

"Stand up, hon," Laurie said. Claire got to her feet and

stood, slick with bathwater, a big smile on her face as Mom soaped down her little private parts.

"I either work those hours or I don't work at all," Laurie said. "There's no halfway."

"Then maybe you shouldn't work at all. Or take a couple of years off and then go back."

"And they'd look at my résumé and ask, 'What did you do for this and that year?'"

"So? You'd tell them you wanted to stay home with your kid."

"Right. And then what happens if we have another one? You think they're going to hire me to manage a major account when there's a possibility I might turn around and leave in a year or two?"

"If they don't, it's discrimination."

"There is no such thing as discrimination in management, darling; there are only qualifications."

The doorbell rang. Stuart went to answer it. The delivery boy was small and swarthy. Stuart took the pizza box and gave him a twenty-dollar bill. The delivery boy turned to go.

"Uh, I was hoping for some change," Stuart said.

The delivery boy grinned. He seemed to be missing every other tooth. "No change."

"Then wait." Stuart opened his wallet: three ones and two twenties. He looked back at the delivery boy. "How can you deliver and not bring any change?"

The boy grinned and shrugged.

"Give me back that twenty and wait here," Stuart said. He went back down the hall to the bathroom and stuck his head in. Claire was bawling as Laurie shampooed her hair. "Nooooooo! Mommy, nooooooo!"

"Have you got a ten?" he shouted.

"Noooo! Noooooo! Nooooooo!"

"Stop splashing, Claire!" Laurie shouted. Then to him: "Look in my wallet."

"Where is it?"

"The bedroom."

He went back down the hall. The delivery boy was standing in the doorway, still grinning. Stuart went into the bedroom and dug Laurie's wallet out of her bag. Inside she had three ones. God, how could she walk around with so little? He looked in the change compartment of the wallet. Two subway tokens and assorted silver. He went back to the door.

"You sure you don't have any change? How can you not have change?"

Grin. "No change."

Stuart reached into his pocket for the twenty. I'll bet he has fifty dollars' worth of change, he thought. But he knows I'm not going to send him back with the pizza and let my family starve.

"Merry Christmas."

The delivery boy took the twenty. "I bring change later."

Stuart took the pizza into the kitchen and put out plates, glasses and napkins. Laurie stopped in the doorway with Claire in her arms, her head a mop of blond strings.

"Pitsa, pitsa!"

"Did you find change?"

He shook his head.

"What did you do?"

"Gave him a twenty."

"I hope it's good," she said.

"My pitsa, my pitsa!" Claire shouted.

"Yes, hon, your pitsa. Let's just get you into your pajamas and then you can have some."

They went down to Claire's room to put on her pajamas and then returned. Laurie placed her in her high chair and cut a piece of pizza into bite-sized pieces. Then she sat down and took a slice for herself.

"Somehow for twenty dollars it doesn't taste as good as it would have for ten," she said.

"Pitsa good, pitsa good!" Claire said, her cheeks already streaked with red tomato sauce.

They both looked at her and smiled.

"Do you think we should have another one?" Stuart asked.

"Not for twenty dollars."

"I meant a baby."

"How?"

"Well, we go to bed together and you don't use any birth control."

"That's not what I meant. I meant how on earth could we deal with another one? Financially, emotionally, in terms of time."

He shrugged. "I just don't think Claire should be an only child."

"Neither do I, but I also don't see how we could do it."

"Where there's a will, there's a way."

"When there's a bill, someone's got to pay."

"Touché."

"Tushy, tushy," Claire said.

They both smiled again.

"She's like a drug," Laurie said.

"So imagine what two would be like."

"An overdose."

Later, in bed.

"I don't know if I'm in the mood."

"Just relax."

"Don't be mad if it doesn't work."

"Think positively."

"I'm thinking about the budget meeting."

The hands of an explosives expert went to work. "We're in the boardroom under the table," he whispered. "Everyone's there. While Peter gives his annual spiel about budget cutbacks, I'm slipping my hand inside your panties."

She giggled, a good sign.

"Martha suggests that Sleepwell could save money by making the Christmas party buffet instead of sit-down. Meanwhile, under the table I'm . . ."

The doorbell rang.

"Who could that be?" she whispered.

"Must be a mistake," he said, but the doorbell rang again.

"Better go see who it is."

Muttering to himself, Stuart got up and pulled on a robe. A minute later he was back.

"Who was it?"

"The pizza delivery boy," he said, sliding back into bed.

"What?"

"He brought the change."

"You're kidding."

"Swear to God."

"It's shocking. Such honesty in this day and age."

"He must have just gotten off the boat," Stuart said, reaching for her. "Now where was I?"

"I'm tired, Woof."

"But a minute ago we were under the board table."

Laurie yawned. "Tomorrow night. I promise."

At 3:30 A.M. he was up, walking through the dark apartment, the prewar wooden floor squeaking under his feet. Was Laurie right? Was it possible that with the mortgage, maintenance, day care and Claire's future education costs they could not afford another baby? Was it conceivable that with the demands of their jobs they simply didn't have enough hours left in the day to raise a second kid? Was the typical yuppie nuclear family destined to be a triad of working parents and an overly pampered only child?

In his dark office he stood by the French doors and parted the curtain. The light in *her* room was on and the white shade was down. He could see her shadow moving back and forth inside. Except for a room on the first floor, hers was the only one lit at that hour. What was she doing? What was her life like? Did she lie awake nights thinking about money? Did she have an IRA? A self-directed Keogh? Term life insurance? Money market and mutual funds? Custodial accounts? A secondary long-distance carrier? Did she pay federal, state and city taxes? Estimated quarterly withholding? Corporate? FUTA? City surcharge? 940s? Unemployment insurance?

The shadow stopped, dead center in the window. The shade rose and *she* leaned her elbows on the windowsill. He could not see her face, only her dark silhouette and the hard yellow light in the room behind her. The next thing he knew, he was walking across his office to the light switch. He flicked it on and returned to the French doors, pulling the curtain open. Then he stood, gazing up at her.

He was certain she could see him now. Just as he could not see her face, he doubted she could see his. They were just two dark silhouettes facing each other in the long walls of brick and dark windows that lined the street. But he wanted her to know he was there.

12

———

"I'M going up there," Eliot said. He was on 0803. It was 2:30 in the afternoon.

"Where?"

"Westchester. I think she's going to see him after work. She just called and said she has to go to a meeting in Stamford and won't be home until late. I know she's seeing him. I have evidence."

"What kind of evidence?"

"I found a note in the garbage a couple of days ago. And last night I found a map in her briefcase. I copied it while she was in the bathroom. I'm going to kill her."

"Uh, Eliot, why don't you just wait until she comes home tonight and talk to her about it?"

"Because she'll lie. She's an incredible liar. State of the art. You can't believe how good she is. The only way I'll ever be sure is to see for myself. I have to go. I'm going."

"How?"

"Hertz."

"What are you going to do if you find them?"

"I already told you."

"You're serious, aren't you?"

"I've had it with all the bullshit. I've had it with everything."

"Can I go with you?"

"What?"

"Let me come along. I'll keep you company."

"Why?"

"Why not?"

He heard nothing but breathing for a moment. "You're trying to stall me."

"How are you getting up there?" Stuart asked.

"The West Side Highway."

"I'll meet you at the Seventy-ninth Street exit. If I'm not there when you get off, get back on and go without me."

"Okay, but I'm not waiting," Eliot said.

Stuart hung up and called Laurie and told her she'd have to pick up Claire that night. Then he turned on his phone machine and went downstairs.

He was standing at the end of the exit ramp when Eliot pulled up in a baby-blue Camaro and rolled down the window. "I've thought it over and I don't want you to come."

Stuart reached for the door handle, but it was locked.

"I'm serious," Eliot said. "This is something I have to do alone." The Camaro started to roll forward.

Stuart jogged alongside the car. "If you don't take me, I'll go back to the house and warn her that you're coming."

"You wouldn't."

"Open the door, Eliot."

"You fuck." Eliot reached across the seat and opened the door. Stuart got in and the Camaro squealed from the curb and shot up Riverside Drive.

"Some friend," Eliot sulked.

"I would rather not have to visit you in prison for the next twenty-five years."

"I wouldn't get that long. I could plead temporary insanity and get it reduced to voluntary manslaughter. I'd be on the street in three. At the most seven."

"With a slightly distended anus."

"Maybe I'd learn to like it. Anything is better than this."

Stuart looked at him. "You frighten me sometimes."

A thin smile appeared on Eliot's lips. "Freedom, my friend, is just another word for nothing left to lose."

They stopped in front of Eliot's building and Eliot jumped out of the car. "Wait here."

Stuart waited. He thought about taking the car and driving away, but Eliot would simply rent another. There was no way to stop him. A few minutes later Eliot burst out of the lobby. "I knew it!" he cried as he got back into the car.

"What?"

With a loud screech, Eliot left rubber down the street. "You want conclusive evidence? I've got it."

"What?"

"There are two tampons missing from the box in the bathroom."

"So?"

"So, she's not having her period."

"So?"

"So, whenever we used to screw, back in prehistoric times that is, she always stuck one in afterward so that nothing leaked."

"Hmm."

"And not only that, but I weighed the tube of contraceptive jelly."

"You *weighed* it?"

"Yeah. Last week I went out and bought a postal scale and I've been weighing it every day. It's down half an ounce."

"I'll say one thing for you, Eliot. You're thorough."

"You ain't seen nothing yet."

They raced up the Henry Hudson and stopped to pay the toll. Eliot asked the toll collector for a receipt.

"Tax-deductible murder?" Stuart asked as they accelerated onto the Saw Mill River Parkway.

"Fuck you," Eliot said. "I can probably expense it." He

reached into his jacket pocket and handed Stuart a wrinkled piece of paper about the size of an index card. "What do you think this is?"

It looked like a shopping list with barely decipherable words written in smudged pencil. There was something about fabric, polyurethane pipe, four-by-fours and a drill bit.

"I don't know."

"It's a love nest."

"What?"

"They've got a place somewhere. It's too expensive to keep shelling out eighty bucks a pop in a motel, so they've found some hole somewhere and they're fixing it up. You know what that means?"

"That you should be committed."

"Fuck you, Stuart. It means that he's married too."

"Or that he still lives with his parents."

Eliot gasped. "What if it's a kid? Like in college or something? That would be the ultimate humiliation."

"Eliot, if I might be frank for a moment. I think your imagination is in overdrive. I still don't understand how we got from this piece of paper to a love nest."

Eliot took the list back and folded it neatly into his pocket. "What else would she be doing with it?"

"How do you even know it's hers?"

"It was in the garbage. Besides, it's her handwriting."

"I can hardly read it. How do you know it's her handwriting?"

"I know," Eliot said.

"Couldn't it possibly be the maid's or someone else who was in the house?"

Eliot shook his head. "I check the garbage every night. No one was in the house the day this appeared."

"Okay, so suppose it's hers. Why does that mean she's building a love nest?"

"A: Because what else do you do with fabric, four-by-fours and polyurethane pipe? B: Because she doesn't even know what the fuck a four-by-four is! He must have dictated it to her." Eliot gripped the wheel tightly and floored the Camaro. The car lurched. "Goddamn them, using my money to build their love nest."

"Calm down, Eliot."

Eliot reached into his jacket again and pulled out another piece of paper. "Look at that."

It looked like a map. Five or six lines, some with street names scrawled next to them. There was a small square with "Ramada Inn" written next to it. And another square that said "the house."

Stuart nodded. "Okay, this looks incriminating. Especially the Ramada Inn."

"No, that's where they held a focus group a couple of Saturdays ago," Eliot said.

"Then it's this thing marked 'the house'?"

"Actually, that's her boss's house. I drove by and checked it out."

"Could she be having an affair with her boss?"

"Not unless she's turned lesbo on me. I guess that's a possibility, but actually, Carol picked her up and gave her a ride to the Ramada Inn that day. I remember she told me that."

"Well, then what's with this map?"

While doing a steady seventy on the Saw Mill, Eliot reached over and pointed to one of the lines. The line led from the Ramada Inn, turned up a street called Park, then veered to the left and off the page. "See that line?"

"Uh-huh."

"It doesn't belong on the map. It has nothing to do with either going to the Ramada Inn or to her boss's house. There's no reason for her to have drawn it."

"So?"

"So it has to be there for a reason. I think it leads to the nest."

"Did you follow it?"

"Yeah, I tried, but it just leads into a residential neighborhood. I think there was another page to this map. Maybe another map he gave her. She said it was an all-day focus group. But think about it. An all-day group on a Saturday? Doesn't it make more sense that it was only half a day and from there she went to the nest? So she drew the roads from this map to where the map he gave her began."

"But you've never seen the other map. You don't even know if it really exists."

Eliot plunged his finger down at the map again. "Then why have this line? It doesn't lead anywhere that she should have gone."

"Eliot, are you aware that you are being almost completely irrational?"

Eliot shook his head. "There are too many loose ends emanating from the central fact that for the last three months she's acted like her greatest wish in life was that I was dead."

"Eliot . . ."

"I'm serious, Stuart, truly serious."

13

———

THE buildings in the office complex where Carol worked looked like huge rectangular spaceships covered with mirrors. Eliot pulled into the parking lot and started to cruise slowly. "There it is."

Stuart saw Eliot's black BMW. Eliot drove past it and then backed into a space three rows away.

"You're going to follow her?"

"You got it."

Stuart looked at his watch. It was just after four. "What if she stays late?"

Eliot smiled. "You said you wanted to keep me company, right?"

"I also want to get home before midnight."

"You will," Eliot said. "One way or the other."

Stuart gazed out at the parking lot. The summer heat wiggled off the tops of the cars. "All she has to do is look in her rearview mirror and she'll see you."

"I'm wearing sunglasses."

"I think there is probable cause to believe that if she looks in her rearview mirror and sees a guy with sunglasses who resembles her husband she may put two and two together."

"Damn. You're right."

"So let's go back to the city and when she gets home tonight you can ask her what she did today. Have a long talk, explain your feelings, ask her to tell you the truth."

Eliot shook his head. "You don't understand, Stuart. If I have to go through one more day of her lies and not knowing what's going on I think I'm going to kill her or myself or both."

"You can't trail her, Eliot. She'll see you."

"You're right." Eliot pushed open the car door and got into the back. He reached over the seat and handed the sunglasses to Stuart. "You'll follow her."

Stuart sat in the driver's seat, wearing the sunglasses, the Camaro's sun visor pulled low. Eliot sat in the back. A remarkable stillness surrounded them. The cars in the parking lot shimmered in the sunlight. Two sea gulls circled lazily in the sky. Now and then a tiny silver speck of a jet passed thousands of feet above.

In the backseat, Eliot sneezed. "Fucking allergies," he mumbled as he pulled out a handkerchief and blew his nose.

"I didn't know you had any," Stuart said.

"Doesn't bother me much in the city." Eliot sniffed. "The pollen count must be a million out here." He blew his nose again. "Jesus."

"What?"

"I don't know. Do you realize that I'm thirty-three years old and this is the first real-life thing that has ever happened to me?"

"What?"

"Up till now everything has been on schedule and according to plan. I grew up, went to college, got a job, got married, got a nice apartment. I mean, I've had my share of petty screw-ups, but basically I've done okay and made decent money. There were no tragedies. No one died. No scandals, no divorces, not even an unexpected illness. My whole family is that way. My sisters, my parents. No one in my family has ever messed up in a major way. What am I going to tell them?"

"You don't have to tell them anything. And there's no reason to think you've messed up."

But it was as if Eliot hadn't heard him. "I never did anything to deserve this, Stu. My whole life I've been good. Really, I swear. The worst thing I ever did was in eleventh grade I got suspended for a day because I pulled the emergency shower ring in the chemistry lab and three hundred gallons of water came out."

"Why did you do that?"

"I don't know. I just had an overwhelming desire to pull it. Haven't you ever had an overwhelming desire to do something crazy?"

Stuart didn't know why, but the image of *her* standing naked on her windowsill popped into his mind. *Just to touch her,* he thought. *To follow her into the night and see.*

"I get them all the time," Eliot went on. "I've spent my whole life trying to fight the urge to do crazy things. After the shower incident I clamped down tight."

"Until today."

"This is not crazy. This is probably the sanest thing I've ever done. At least now I'll know for certain."

"So what happened in chemistry?"

Eliot sniffed and blew his nose. "I got a C. Pulled my grade point average down three-tenths of a point that semester and for all I know that's why I didn't get accepted at a better college."

"Sounds a little farfetched."

"You're wrong, Stu. Things like that follow you your whole life. One day you're competing against another bank on a big deal and it turns out their lawyer is a kid you went to high school with and he remembers that you're the idiot who pulled the emergency shower ring in the chem lab.

The next thing you know, you're out of the deal and flying home with a crummy time-and-effort fee."

"That's happened?"

"Not yet. But I swear I lie awake some nights wondering when it will. There she is."

Stuart looked across the parking lot and saw Carol, wearing a gray skirt and a pale blouse. She was walking in high heels, not entirely graceful in them. They watched her cross the lot, opening her purse as she went and taking out a pair of sunglasses. There was something fascinating about watching her when she was unaware of them, Stuart thought. It was like seeing a Carol he'd never seen before. This wasn't Eliot's wife; this was a businesswoman. It was something he'd often wished he could do with Laurie— view her in her business environment and see how different or similar she was from the Laurie he knew at home.

Stuart reached for the ignition.

"Don't start the engine until she's in the car," Eliot whispered as he ducked down behind the seat.

Stuart waited and watched as Carol stopped beside the BMW and reached into her bag for her keys. Could she possibly be having an affair? He tried to imagine what it must have been like, trying to keep it secret not only from Eliot, but from her friends and fellow workers as well. What he imagined was excitement, a feeling of being incredibly alive and filled with the emotional highs and lows he seemed to have left behind in marriage. *Till death do you part.* Thinking about his life with Laurie, Stuart wondered if just a little part of him had already died, that little part that felt the excitement of a new relationship and the thrill of a new touch. To think that he would never feel that again made life seem terribly finite. It was one more fabulous sensation, like losing your virginity, and getting your first big account, that he would never be allowed to feel again.

If that was what motivated Carol and her alleged lover, then while Stuart would hate them both for what they were

91

doing to Eliot, somewhere deep inside he would also feel just a glimmer of understanding.

Carol got into the BMW. Stuart waited until she closed the door, and then turned the key.

"Try to stay as far back as you can," Eliot whispered.

The BMW headed toward the exit. Stuart followed slowly behind. Carol made a left onto Boston Post Road.

"Which way are we going?" Eliot whispered.

"East on Boston Post Road," Stuart whispered back. The BMW stopped at a light and he slowed the Camaro down and stopped behind it.

"What's happening?" Eliot whispered.

"We're stopped at a light," he whispered back.

"Where is she?"

"Right in front of us."

"Jesus," Eliot hissed. "Don't get too close."

"There are no cars between us," Stuart whispered back. "What am I supposed to do?"

"Is she looking in the rearview mirror?"

"No."

"What's she doing?"

"She's waiting for the light to change. And why are we whispering?"

"Christ, I don't know," Eliot said, returning to his normal voice.

"Where did she say the meeting was?" Stuart asked.

"Stamford."

"Which way is that?"

"The way we're going."

They followed her to a drugstore in a small shopping center and parked in front of a dry cleaner two doors down.

"What's going on?" Eliot asked.

"She just went into the drugstore."

"Great, might as well take a nap. She'll have to try twenty-six different shades of lipstick before she leaves."

But she was out two minutes later and got back in the

BMW. Eliot sneezed and blew his nose again. "Geez, that was fast. She must be late for the meeting."

Stuart glanced over the seat at him. "I thought the whole point of this expedition was to see if she was meeting her lover."

"Well, she wouldn't tell me she was having a meeting in Stamford if that was where she was meeting him. She'd say Armonk or Harrison or someplace. She's too good at covering her tracks."

"Does that mean we can turn around and go back to the city?"

Eliot slumped back low in the rear seat and rubbed his nose in the handkerchief. "Jesus, I don't know. I guess."

"How do I do it?"

"Make a right at the next light. Shit, Stuart, I feel like an idiot taking you on this wild-goose chase. I must be out of my mind to think that Carol would be cheating on me. What a shit I am. Here she is working her butt off for us and I think she's spending her afternoons in the sack."

Ahead of them, the BMW made a right turn. Eliot looked over the seat and laughed. "Now we can't even get away from her."

Both cars headed south. In the distance Stuart could see the entrance ramp to the New England Thruway. The ramp was on the right and just before it was a Motel Six and a Shell station. A line of cars including the BMW was drifting into the right lane to get onto the thruway. Stuart watched the cars behind him in the rearview mirror and moved over. A few seconds later he was on the entrance ramp, accelerating onto the thruway.

"We should be back just in time for you to return the car and catch the subway home," he said.

In the back, Eliot didn't answer.

"Eliot?"

"She didn't get on the thruway."

Stuart looked at the cars ahead and behind them and saw

no sign of the BMW. "Well, if she was going to Stamford she would have gone straight under the underpass and then gotten on going east."

"She didn't."

"Then what . . . ?"

"Get off at the next exit," Eliot said.

"Why?"

"She's still back there."

"Where?"

"At that motel."

"Eliot, seriously. We've taken this trip. You've thrown off some of your demons. Now let's get back to the city and forget about it, okay?"

"Go back," Eliot said.

"I'm sorry, but I've had enough. I'm going home."

Stuart felt two hands go around his neck and begin to squeeze. "Listen to me," Eliot said behind him, his lips close to Stuart's ear. "You are my best friend and I love you like a brother, but if you don't get off at the next exit I am going to start to choke you and if you let go of the wheel and try to stop me we'll probably crash and die and frankly right now I couldn't give a shit."

"I'll just pull off the road and stop," Stuart said.

"Good. Then I'll get out and walk back," Eliot said, tightening his grip.

Stuart started to choke. "Stop it, Eliot."

"Are you going to turn around?"

He began to cough. Eliot's fingertips were crushing his Adam's apple. He couldn't breath. "Okay, Eliot, okay."

It was a bleak-looking two-story prefab concrete building painted yellow with brown trim on the doors and window frames. A pickup truck and a Toyota were parked in front.

"Go around back," Eliot said.

Stuart steered the car around to the back of the motel. The asphalt became loose and full of potholes. A step van with no tires sat rusting in the sun. Down at the end of the parking lot, outside one of the last units, two cars were parked. The black BMW and a gold Mercedes.

Stuart stopped the Camaro. His breath grew short as he wondered if Eliot would try anything crazy. But his friend stayed in the back and said nothing. Stuart glanced at him in the rearview mirror. Eliot was sitting up straight, his lips parted and his eyes almost glazed—a look of near pure in-credulity. For a long time they sat and stared at the two parked cars. In the trees near the step van a cicada chirped. On the second floor of the motel, a black housekeeper in a light-blue uniform came out of one unit and let herself into the one next to it. Eliot sniffed and blew his nose. Stuart didn't know what to do or say. He felt incredibly bad. Twice more he glanced into the rearview mirror at the backseat. Both times Eliot was motionless, leaning forward, staring out the window.

Finally Stuart said, "It's not going to do any good to just sit here."

"Wait," Eliot said.

"Why?"

"You know what that is? It's a fucking Five-Sixty SEC."

"The car?"

"Thing must be brand new." Eliot pushed the passenger seat forward and started to get out.

"Where're you going?"

"I just want to see something."

"Eliot . . ."

"Don't worry, I won't bother them."

Stuart watched him cross the parking lot. He kept his hand on the door handle, prepared to leap out and stop him from doing anything crazy. Eliot stopped next to the sleek gold sedan and stared at it for a moment. Then he reached down and picked up a loose chunk of asphalt from the ground.

The screech of stone against metal broke the stillness as Eliot etched a thin black squiggle along the car's side. Stuart jumped out of the Camaro, took two quick steps, but then stopped. Something in his head wouldn't let him interfere yet. Maybe it was the feeling of how unfair it all was. Or knowing that this was probably the only revenge Eliot would ever have. Whatever the reason, he let Eliot circle the car twice, leaving his indelible marks on the hood and trunk as well, and didn't suggest that it might be time to go until Eliot had etched I AM A SCUMBAG on the roof.

They rode back to the city without talking. Stuart double-parked in front of his building. Eliot was slumped in the passenger seat, the tips of his fingers pressed into the corners of his eyes.

"Think you can take it from here?" Stuart asked.

"Yeah." Eliot started to slide over into the driver's seat.

"Sure you're okay?"

"Uh huh."

"If you need anything or feel like talking . . ."

Eliot nodded. Not knowing what else to say, Stuart started toward the sidewalk.

"Hey, you know what it was like?" Eliot called from the window.

Stuart turned. "Like pulling the ring in the chem lab?"

Eliot smirked. "Eight times better."

14

IT was ninety-four degrees outside and humid. Stuart sat at his desk wearing a pair of tennis shorts and no shirt. A small plastic fan on top of the Quotron blew on him, but it wasn't strong enough to keep the beads of sweat from forming on his forehead and rolling down the bridge of his nose. He stood up and went to the French doors. Across the street the young gay man with the tattoo on his shoulder was getting it from his lover again. *Her* shade was still down.

The phone tweeted. Stuart looked back at his desk. He knew it was Eliot.

"Hello?"

"We talked about it," Eliot said.

"What did she say?"

"She says she's mad that I fucked up his car and she's in love with him and she's sorry that she has to hurt me."

"What did you say?"

"I said I was sorry too, and if I had it all to do over again I'd still fuck up his car."

"What is she going to do?"

"She doesn't know."

"What are you going to do?"

"I'm going to see a divorce lawyer at four this afternoon."

"God, Eliot, I'm sorry."

"Even when I was certain she was cheating on me, I never really believed it. I guess I didn't want to believe it."

"Who would?"

"Well, it's done now. It's kind of a relief. She knows I know. No more lies."

"Maybe it would be better if you got out of the house for a while. You want to stay with us?"

"It's all been worked out."

"What's been worked out?"

"I'm going to stay at my grandfather's place for a couple of weeks."

"Your grandfather's place? Your grandfather lives in a nursing home."

"Yeah, but my aunt took him to her house in New Jersey for the month so his bed's available."

"Eliot, you cannot stay in a nursing home. I absolutely forbid it. It's the most ridiculous thing I've ever heard."

"It's not so bad. They clean up the room and make your meals. They said they'd even keep my dinner warm until I get home from work."

"That is the craziest thing I've ever heard. Here you are breaking up with your wife and you're going to go live with a bunch of incontinent old people? You'll probably kill yourself."

"I figure if I can live through this I can live through anything."

"Come stay with us, please."

"I'll think about it. I'll talk to the lawyer at four. Maybe I'll talk to you after that."

"Eliot, are you sure you're going to be okay? Want me to go to the lawyer with you?"

"Thanks, man, but I'll be fine."

"You sure?"

"Hey, I'm walking, I'm talking and I haven't killed anyone yet, have I?"

"Okay, but promise to call me."

"Don't worry, I will."

He managed to get a few hours of work done, and then went to IFIL. Claire was lying on a cot in a corner of the room. She looked pale and was not wearing the same clothes she'd gone to school in that morning.

"She had three attacks of diarrhea," Sam said gravely. "We usually send them home, but she had the third so late in the afternoon that we decided to keep her until you came."

Stuart put her in the stroller and wheeled her home. Claire was listless. She cried when he took her temperature. She had a fever of 102.8.

He called the doctor, who told him to give her baby Tylenol, clear liquids and Pedialyte. He set her up on the couch with a cotton blanket and put on the *Sesame Street* tape. Then he called Laurie and told her not to worry, but Claire was a little sick. She said she'd come right home.

At 7:15, in the middle of dinner, the phone rang. Stuart answered it. "Hello?"

"Hello, this is Alice Messing, Melissa's mother."

"Oh, hi."

"I heard Claire had the diarrhea today."

"That's right."

"You know why, don't you?" Mrs. Messing said.

"Uh, I'm not sure that I do."

"Billy Gretzinger. His sister is in the threes class and he caught it from her three weeks ago. His mother only kept him home for one day. He was still sick when she sent him back and now all the other twos have caught it, except my Melissa."

"I didn't know that."

"I think it's awful," Mrs. Messing said. "Completely irresponsible of her to send Billy back to school and infect other children."

"Well, the kids always catch things from each other, don't they?" Stuart said.

"Only because parents are too selfish to keep their children home until they're past the infectious stage. I know you wouldn't dream of sending Claire back until she's completely better."

"We'll keep her out until the doctor says she can go back. But we can't keep her home forever. It's hard to find someone to take care of her during the day."

"I don't have to remind you that school policy states that a child should not come back to school until at least twenty-four hours after the last sign of fever."

"Yes, I was aware of that," Stuart said.

"I think you should call Mrs. Gretzinger and tell her that the next time she sends Billy to school sick you're going to bring the matter up with the director."

"I'm still not convinced that Claire caught it from Billy."

"He was the first child in the twos class to have this bug," Mrs. Messing told him. "I watch these things very carefully."

"Well, I appreciate your concern," Stuart said.

"Thank you," Mrs. Messing said. "And I hope Claire feels better. I look forward to seeing her again next week."

"Uh, it's only Tuesday," Stuart said. "Even if we keep Claire home two days there's still a chance she'll be back on Friday."

"I'd hate to see her come back before she was ready," Mrs. Messing said.

"So would I, Mrs. Messing. Now good-bye." Stuart hung up.

"Who was that?" Laurie asked.

"Mrs. Messing making sure we don't send Claire back to school until she's better."

"God, she has balls."

"I can't figure out how she could be so certain that poor

little Billy Gretzinger is the one who's responsible," Stuart said. "I mean, what is she? A medical detective?"

"Neurotic is more like it," Laurie said. "She probably feels terrible that she isn't staying home like her mother and grandmother before her. So she tries to control the situation from the outside. If Melissa becomes sick, she'll feel she isn't being a good mother. So she'll do anything to keep Melissa well."

"Do you feel that way?" he asked.

"Sometimes," Laurie said. "I keep telling myself that little kids have to get sick, especially kids in day care. It's all part of developing an immune system. But every time Claire comes home wearing some other kid's socks, or I discover that Sam's gotten the nipples on the bottles mixed up, I just want to yank her out of there and keep her home for good."

"Maybe we could get Betty back now that Howard is moving."

"I couldn't trust her now," Laurie said.

"What do we do about the next couple of days?" Stuart asked.

"I'll start calling baby-sitters after dinner."

All his life the phrase "dishpan hands" had been an abstract concept until the day he'd discovered that his hands were cracked and dry. Partially it was because Laurie insisted on using plates even when they ate takeout. Partially it was because Claire's plastic dishes and bowls tended to melt in the dishwasher and so had to be washed by hand. While Laurie called around for a baby-sitter, Stuart squeezed some Ivory into the sink and turned on the hot water. He rolled up his sleeves and started to tug on a pair of pink Playtex gloves. He had yet to find a brand of latex gloves that fit comfortably. It was obvious that the companies who made these gloves did not feel there was enough demand to warrant a line of men's sizes.

Stuart got both gloves on and started to wash the dishes.

It was a Tuesday night. Were he still at Bingham he probably would have worked all day at the office and then caught a flight to Chicago or Washington or Atlanta. He'd probably have checked into a Ritz-Carlton or Four Seasons hotel and would just be sitting down to dinner with a client at one of the best restaurants in town. Somehow, when he'd given all that up to work for himself and spend more time with his family, he hadn't factored in the dishes.

15

_____

H E called to wish his father a happy birthday. Mr. Miller wasn't at the club, so Stuart tried the house. The maid answered and said he wasn't there so Stuart tried the car.

"Hello?"

"Hi, Dad, where are you?"

"On the Hutch."

"Going to the club?"

"Yep. Thought I'd get in eighteen this afternoon."

"Well, happy birthday."

"Thanks. I don't feel sixty."

"Who knows what sixty is supposed to feel like?"

"I sure as hell don't. I swear to God, Stuart, I feel younger today than I have in the last twenty years."

"Why do you think that is?"

"Don't know. Maybe it's because you're all grown up and on your own, I'm financially set, and my handicap is down to fifteen."

"Dad, I've been on my own since college, you've been

financially set for at least ten years and your handicap has always been under seventeen."

"Well, then it must be something else."

"So, Laurie and I have the same question we ask every year. We know you have everything, but is there anything you can think of that you might want for a present?"

"How about something around twenty-two, blond and built like Yvette Mimieux?"

"Who?"

"You don't know who Yvette Mimieux is?"

"Sorry."

"Well, then I guess that's not who I want for my birthday present."

"Dad, is there a nonflesh present you might like?"

"I'll be honest with you, Stuart, there really isn't. At this point in my life I get joy from three things. Following the market, playing golf and looking at young women."

"Did you get any responses from your ad?"

"A few, but mostly from young ladies with names like Joy, Brandy and Candy."

"Did you and Mom work things out?"

"Stuart, your mother and I worked things out years ago. You know, there was a great movie on last night. *The Thomas Crown Affair.*"

Stuart had a vague recollection. "Steve McQueen and Faye Dunaway. They play chess and fly around in a glider."

"It has one of the greatest sex scenes I can recall," his father said.

Stuart could not remember the sex scene, but talking with his father about sex made him uncomfortable. It seemed to be very much on both their minds, except his father constantly talked about it and he didn't. He didn't see the point in talking about it. It seemed crass and didn't make anything better anyway.

"Can you think of anything, Dad?"

"Suppose I come in one evening and take everyone to dinner," his father said.

"That's not a present to you."

"Of course it is. It's a joy to see you."

"Suppose we take you to dinner," Stuart said.

"Okay, fine. How about next Thursday?"

"See you then."

On Thursday, his father called on the intercom from downstairs.

"Come on up," Stuart said.

"First come down and see my new car," his father said.

Stuart took the elevator down. His father was waiting on the sidewalk, wearing a white cap, a yellow cardigan sweater and lime-green slacks. Double-parked on the street was a new white Chrysler Le Baron convertible with a red interior.

"Pretty snazzy car, Dad," Stuart said.

"It's my midlife Chrysler," Mr. Miller said.

Stuart smiled. "Tell me you bought the car just so you could use that line."

"You don't like it?"

"No, it's fine," Stuart said. "I like it."

Stuart's grandfather had had two sons: Stuart's father, Nathan, and his uncle, Willy. Nathan had run a dress showroom in the garment district for twenty years, providing Stuart with a comfortable middle-class childhood. Willy had gone to medical school and moved to Los Angeles to become a bachelor neurosurgeon. Stuart used to see Willy once a year around Christmas. He remembered him as a chubby, jovial man with smooth skin and red cheeks.

One day about ten years ago Willy was stabbed to death in his house by a young man described in the *Los Angeles*

Times as a cocaine addict and "former acquaintance." Three months later, Stuart's father sold his showroom and retired. He had inherited two million dollars from Willy. Stuart knew this because his father put him in charge of managing the estate. It was Stuart's first account. He was twenty-four years old.

They went to a new restaurant which had opened in the spot where the last lumberyard on the Upper West Side below Eighty-sixth Street had once been. The restaurant had a long, mirror-lined bar, large pots of flowers, and very attractive waitresses. Stuart thought his father would enjoy it.

They sat Claire in a booster seat and fed her bits from their own dinners.

Stuart's father leaned toward Laurie. "So tell me, how's work?"

Laurie rolled her eyes in the familiar gesture. "Too busy."

"Why?" Mr. Miller asked.

"Oh, you don't want to know," Laurie said.

"Yes, I do," Stuart's father said, resting his elbows on the table. "I miss talking about business. I'd love to hear."

Stuart was surprised to see Laurie smile. She seemed flattered. "Well, for one thing we're trying to push a big promotion for Pillow Market in November."

"Pillow Market?"

"That's when all the pillow buyers come to New York to buy pillows," Stuart said.

"We want every buyer to have a Sleepwell pillow in their hotel room," Laurie said. "It's a logistical nightmare."

"I can imagine," Mr. Miller said. "You'll have to track down every reservation at every hotel in town."

"Oh, no, we can't possibly do that," Laurie said. "We're starting an ad campaign with an 800 number. If a buyer wants a pillow all they have to do is call and we'll make the arrangements with the hotels."

Mr. Miller nodded. "That makes sense."

"The problem is getting the hotels to put the pillows in the right rooms on the right nights," Laurie said. "Also, the Down Association is making a big push to increase their market share."

"You don't make down pillows?" Stuart's father asked.

Laurie shook her head. "All our pillows are fiberfill."

"The problem with down," Stuart said, "is the big down payment."

Both his father and Laurie looked at him. Neither laughed.

"And on top of all that," Laurie said, "the price of fiber is going up and we can't pass the cost on to the consumer. So our profits are dropping, plus we have to spend a lot on this new promotion."

"And your boss doesn't like it," Mr. Miller said.

Stuart could have added that the Sleepwell shareholders didn't like it either, but he didn't. He was already feeling like a third wheel. His father kept asking about Laurie's career. In fact, he seemed captivated, sincerely or otherwise, by what any attractive woman under the age of forty had to say. Laurie responded animatedly, which Stuart found curious considering her earlier characterization of his father as a letch. Apparently that meant he was charming in public, but dangerous in private. While they talked, Stuart ate his dinner and made sure Claire didn't launch her spoon across the dining room. He wondered if his father would ask about *his* career.

Claire behaved well through dinner, but just before dessert she started to whine and rub her eyes.

"Sleepy," Laurie said.

"No!" Claire banged her little fist against the tablecloth. "Not sleepy!"

But a few moments later her eyes began to close and her head rolled forward for a second before she caught herself.

"I better take her home," Laurie said, pushing her chair back.

"We'll all go," Stuart's father said.

"It's not necessary," Laurie said as she got up. "It's a nice night. Why don't you take a walk on Columbus Avenue and get some ice cream?"

"You sure?" Stuart asked.

"As long as you bring a little treat home for me." Laurie picked up Claire, who immediately put her head on her mother's shoulder and closed her eyes. Stuart and his father got up and kissed them both good-bye.

Stuart paid the check. He and his father left the restaurant and walked toward Columbus. It was a warm, comfortable evening with an air-quality index that was probably above average for that time of year. The sidewalks were crowded with people who appeared to be doing nothing more important than strolling, as if they'd temporarily forgotten that the normal pace on New York City sidewalks was about the same as race walking.

Mr. Miller lit a cigarette. After years of arguing, Stuart had given up trying to get him to quit.

"So how do you like working at home?" Mr. Miller asked.

"It's good, Dad. I see a lot more of Claire and Laurie. It's incredible to watch Claire grow."

"And you feel you can stay on top of things?"

"Of course. Why not?"

"Well, you're out of the action now."

"Dad, I'm only eighty blocks from the action. I've got the Quotron and the computer and I'm on the phone all day. Just because I'm not physically present doesn't mean I'm not there."

His father tended to hold the cigarette high between his index and middle fingers, almost between the fingertips. It had always struck Stuart as an effeminate gesture, and bothered him almost as much as the smoking did. "What I always admired about you, Stuart, was your intuitive feel for the market. Your hunches have been excellent. I guess I worry that being off the Street you're going to lose the opportunity to use your intuitive abilities."

Stuart looked at his father. "I can't believe I'm hearing this, Dad. Are you unhappy with the returns I've gotten you?"

"No, but I'm concerned about the future. Yours and mine. You want to know why I had that damn showroom on Seventh Avenue all those years? You want to know why I took that damn train five days a week, month after month, year after year? Because I knew I had to be there, not trying to run a business out of my living room. I'll tell you something I learned very early in life, Stuart. New York is a tough town. If you want to swim in these waters, you either become a shark or you get devoured."

"But it's different now, Dad. Everything is computerized. I get the news just as fast as anyone else."

"The real news doesn't come over computers," Mr. Miller said. "The real news is whispered across lunch tables."

They walked in silence for a few blocks, Stuart trying to gather his wits. He had come to expect staunch support from his father. Not only that, but his father's was the largest single account he had.

They stopped at Columbus Avenue's newest ice-cream franchise and got scoops of vanilla with chunks of cookies and caramel in them. Stuart bought a large chocolate-chip cookie for Laurie.

"I didn't mean to put the fear of the Lord in you," his father said as they stepped back out onto the sidewalk. "I just wanted you to know that I'm concerned. I think your judgment is sound and I'm sure you'll be the first to realize if your business is being hurt by this new arrangement. Now look at that."

Coming down the sidewalk toward them was a tall blond

woman walking an Afghan hound. The woman was wearing an oversized white V-neck T-shirt and no brassiere. Her breasts bounced under the shirt as the dog pulled at the leash.

"Mother of God," his father mumbled.

Stuart felt better. They were back on familiar ground. The woman and dog passed them. Mr. Miller stared at her. Stuart noticed that his father's ice-cream cone was beginning to drip. "Better lick it, Dad."

"I would if I could."

"The ice cream, Dad."

Mr. Miller wiped his fingers with a napkin. "Where do women like that come from?" he asked.

"They are sent here to remind us that we are mortal," Stuart said.

"If only I were young and single again," his father said with a sigh.

Stuart wondered if he would someday regret whatever it was his father regretted. Then it occurred to him that perhaps he already did. Was admiring younger women, or at least regretting that they did not admire him, part of a male rite of passage that began in one's thirties and persisted until the hormones gave out? Oddly, Stuart recalled that in his early twenties, right after college, he had gone through a period when he had been more attracted to older women than to women his own age. He was just starting out on his own and the idea of a more mature and established woman must have appealed to him because he'd dated several, and had a reasonably long relationship with one, a thirty-six-year-old art dealer who lived in SoHo with her five-year-old daughter. After eight months of practically spending every night with him, the woman began to hint that he should move in. Stuart was reluctant, and shortly thereafter was once again sleeping alone.

So now it was younger women. Of course, he was still in love with Laurie and still found women of all ages attractive, but there was something about women in their early twenties that definitely brought out those carnal impulses. God knew women's rights advocates would have a field day with him, and he was a bit ashamed to find himself thinking so chauvinistically. But these were the honest impulses inside of him, and no amount of apologizing or rationalizing seemed to quell them.

His father finished his ice cream and lit another cigarette. They started to walk home. "Are you thinking about having another child?"

"We think about it, but we haven't decided."

"It'll be good for her to have a brother or sister."

Stuart looked at his father. "Don't you think I turned out okay?"

His father laughed. "Of course I do. I'm just saying, in the best of all worlds . . ."

"How come you didn't have more?"

"I always wanted to but your mother said you were enough."

"Was it a bad pregnancy?"

"Any pregnancy was a bad pregnancy to your mother."

"Well, I watched Laurie go through labor and I have to admit it's pretty rough."

His father gave him a disgusted look. "Your generation . . . What do you think would happen if every woman felt that way?"

"There'd be a lot of only children in the world," Stuart said.

They turned off Columbus and headed toward West End.

"So how are things with Mom?" Stuart asked.

"No different."

"What does that mean?"

"It means we're two strangers sharing a house. We don't talk to each other. We hardly look at each other."

"How did it get that way?"

111

"I sometimes wonder that myself," his father said. "I'm not sure I know. The resentment just builds and builds until you can hardly be civil with each other."

"The resentment?"

His father nodded.

"What do you resent?" Stuart asked.

His father glanced at him. "It's hard to put into words."

"Would you try?"

The doorman opened the door and they walked into the lobby of his building. Stuart pushed the button for the elevator and they watched the floor numbers light up as the elevator came down. The doors opened. A woman and a boy walked out. The boy was carrying a plastic machine gun. Stuart and his father got in.

"Someday we'll sit down and talk about it," Mr. Miller said. "It's a long complicated matter and I couldn't explain it to you in an elevator."

That night Stuart lay in bed in the dark wondering, What was it that made a man always yearn to touch yet another woman? Insecurity? The need to know that he was still attractive? What did the prototypical strong silent married male do about it? Bear the burden in silence, sublimating his temptations into the good old Protestant work ethic? No, he probably had an affair. But Stuart loved Laurie. Could you have an affair without it affecting your relationship with your wife and child? He doubted it. Besides, he didn't need an affair. He needed something purely physical. Something that happened once. Or maybe twice. Just for variety. A prostitute? God, no. That was far too demeaning and impersonal. What he needed was someone friendly. Someone who fit between an affair and a prostitute.

Her?

He pictured himself in her sun-drenched room, spent, relaxed, lounging against the large throw pillows that were

112

her only furniture. And, of course, she was there, attentive, her head resting on his stomach, her hands smoothing the hair on his legs. Her room was a place beyond moral judgment. A place where the pressures of work, husbanding, and parenting were suspended. A place of infinite variety where every meal was home-cooked.

Childhood, he thought. That's what it was. Childhood, with sex.

PART
TWO

PART
TWO

16

___

SHE was aware of him. He was sure of it. Sometimes in the afternoons he would stand by the French doors and she would go to her window and glance down at him. At first he was startled and jumped away, letting the curtains close. But soon he grew bolder and stood his ground, only averting his eyes downward when he saw her, as if he was looking at something in the street and didn't know she was there. Sometimes he stood like that for half an hour, his face turned down toward the street, but his eyes periodically darting upward to see if she was at the window. Sometimes she would be there the entire time, also gazing down to the street. Sometimes he thought she snuck peeks at him too.

He bought a pair of binoculars, but for several days was too timid to use them. To stand by the doors looking out at the world through the naked eye was understandable, explainable—his eyes needed a rest from reading reports and staring at VDTs. He wanted to see if the mailman had gotten to his block yet. He enjoyed looking at the clouds, the sky, the activity on the street.

But to stand at the doors with binoculars meant only one thing. He was a Peeping Tom. A pervert.

So he first tried them at night while Laurie gave Claire a bath.

He stood in his office in the dark, and witnessed a bonanza. Not with the woman on the ninth floor, but in a room on the third. The lights were on and the shade was up, and through the binoculars he could see the standard wooden dresser and lamp inside. Beyond that was a closet and the door. He could not see the bed, but he was certain it was to the left of the window. To the right he could see the edge of the bathroom door.

As he watched, a young, chubby, dark-haired woman made several trips in the nude across his line of sight, going in and out of the bathroom. At one point she turned her head, nodded and said something to someone he could not see, someone who was probably on the bed.

There was a longer pause while she was out of sight. Stuart waited, his fingers nervously turning the focus wheel on the binoculars. Sometimes Laurie gave Claire a quick bath, and he didn't want to be discovered. He was almost ready to give up when the young woman appeared again, going into the bathroom. Why so many trips? What could she be doing in there?

Then something else caught his eye. It came from the left side of the room. Just a slight movement, something small and dark and gradually growing longer, jiggling slightly as it grew. It had a bit of an arch to it.

Could it be?

Stuart adjusted the focus. Unbelievable.

It was attached to a black man. An older black man. Old enough possibly to be her father. *Or grandfather!* And, although his observations in the field were limited, Stuart was certain that it was longer than any white man's he had ever seen.

The black man was wearing a lime-green shirt. Below its tails two splendly black legs shuffled slowly toward the bathroom. His pants must have been down around his ankles.

He stopped right in front of the window. Just stopped there and took his dick in his hand and wagged it up and down like the arm on a car jack. He was talking to the girl. She came out of the bathroom. He said something and she said something. Then he pointed down and she looked down at it and nodded. Then he said something more and she nodded again.

What in God's name could they be talking about?

The black man turned and shuffled back toward the bed. The young woman reached for the shade and pulled it down. Stuart heard the little pitter-patter of feet coming down the hall from the bathroom. He put the binoculars away.

Claire conked out early that night. Laurie put her in the crib and came into the living room where Stuart was reading.

"I thought I smelled gas in the kitchen," she said.

"I'll check." Stuart went into the kitchen. He didn't smell it. He checked the pilot light, but it was lit. When he came out, Laurie was sitting on the couch, thumbing through *The New Yorker.*

"Didn't smell it," he said, easing down onto the couch beside her.

"Hmm."

"Feel like going into the bedroom?" Stuart asked.

"Isn't it early?"

"We don't have to go to sleep afterward."

"Hmm."

"So?"

Laurie let the magazine fall to her lap. "I don't know, Woof. I can't just get up and go into the bedroom and perform. I have to get in the mood."

He leaned over and kissed her on the neck, crooning softly. *"I'm in the mood for luuuuvvvve. Simply because you're near meeeeee."*

Laurie let her head go back. "Woof, could we get a movie?"

He sat up. "That makes me feel great. Here I am trying to be romantic, trying to get you in the mood, and all you want to do is watch a movie."

"A porno movie."

He stared at her. Was this *his* wife Laurie? The woman he had lived with for the last seven years? A woman who would not wear a two-piece bathing suit to the beach? Who disapproved of changing Claire's diaper in public? A woman who thought Plato's Retreat was an old-age home for philosophers?

"Stop staring at me," she said. "I just thought it might help."

"Help what?"

"Help put me in the mood."

Well, in *that* case, he thought. But still . . .

"I can't," he said.

"Why not?"

"I can't go into the Video Connection and ask for a porno movie. They *know* me there."

"So?"

"So it's embarrassing."

It was her turn to stare at him. She started to laugh. "Oh, Woof, you are funny."

"Really? Well, if you want to watch a porno movie so much, you go get it."

She shook her head.

"Suppose we go together," he said.

"We can't leave Claire."

He shrugged. "So much for that idea."

"Wait, there's a place on Seventy-second Street."

He got there ten minutes before closing time. Inside at least half a dozen people were waiting to get movies. Stuart decided to wait outside until it emptied out, but as closing time approached, the store only got more crowded. What was worse, two teenagers were behind the counter. Both clean-cut, private-school types. One a girl wearing a red Polo shirt, the other a boy in a light-blue Oxford.

At 9:29 he went in and stood in front of the boy, who was busy writing up an order.

"Can I help you?" the girl called from down the counter.

"That's okay. I'll wait."

"We're closing," she said.

"Uh, yeah."

The boy looked up from the order. "Can I help you, sir?"

"Well, uh, I was looking for a movie."

"What movie?"

"I'm not quite sure."

"New release? Comedy? Drama? Mystery? Cartoon?"

"Uh, X-rated," Stuart said in a low voice, aware that a man and woman were waiting behind him.

"You know the title?"

"No."

"Who's in it?"

"I don't know that either. I don't have a precise one in mind."

The kid reached under the counter and pulled out a thick, dog-eared catalogue about the size of a phone book entitled, *Adult Movie Guide*. A photomontage of scantily clad women leered at him from the cover.

"You've got all your titles here, a description of each movie, cross-referenced to the stars and predominant theme," the boy said.

Stuart hastily pushed the catalogue away. "I, uh, was looking for something that a couple might enjoy. Something that isn't, you know, offensive to women."

The boy took the catalogue back and turned to the girl, speaking in a loud voice for all the customers in the store to hear. "Amy, what do we have on the adult list that a couple would enjoy and that isn't offensive to women?"

Stuart stared down at the counter, feeling every eye in the store on him. He was totally mortified and would have

121

gladly given his left hand to become invisible at that moment. Amy turned to a shelf of cassettes behind her and pulled one out. "How about *Deep in Paradise*?"

"Okay, great," Stuart mumbled. He would have taken *Bambi* just to get out of that store.

"It was the single most humiliating experience in recent memory," he said later as he loaded the tape into the VCR.

"Why?" Laurie asked.

"Imagine asking a kid for a porno movie you and your wife can watch."

"That's what you said?"

"I know, I know. It probably didn't matter. For all I know every pervert in the city says that when he takes out a dirty movie."

"You were really that embarrassed?"

"Yes. I don't know why, but I was. I felt like there was going to be a special bulletin on the eleven-o'clock news showing me leaving Video World with *Deep in Paradise* in my hands."

She laughed.

"If you think it's so funny," he said. "You can return it tomorrow."

For the first time since Claire was born and Laurie added the title of Mother/Caretaker to Lover, Wife and Executive, Stuart felt like he was discovering a new facet of her personality. Laurie—mother, lover, wife, executive, and watcher of porno movies. It was something he could never have suggested, although it was a standard fantasy of his and, he believed, of most other men—to make love to one woman while watching another. A double bonus.

Laurie suggested he spread a blanket out on the floor in the living room in front of the television while she went into the bedroom. She returned wearing the black teddy he had given her on Valentine's Day the year they'd been married. He stripped to his underwear and they settled down on the blanket together to watch *Deep in Paradise* starring a young redhead named Paradise Ali.

It began with a surprise. There *were* white men who compared to the black gentleman across the street. Stuart had not been concerned about size for years, not since high school when, he had been relieved to see in the showers, he appeared to be within the acceptable parameters.

But what had happened since then? Had he somehow fallen behind?

"No, silly, you're perfectly fine," Laurie giggled, fondling him. "Did you think men with average penises get jobs in porno movies?"

"I never really thought about it."

"They always have big penises."

"How do you know?"

"I had a boyfriend in college whose idea of a date on Friday night was to take me to the porno movie house in Schenectady."

"You never told me that."

"It never came up."

Stuart stared at her. "I can't believe you used to go to porno movies in college. Did he try to make you do stuff in the theater or something?"

"He suggested it a few times, but I wasn't interested."

"Why not?"

"Really, Stuart, in a movie theater?"

Well, he supposed not. Meanwhile, on the television, Ms. Ali was pulling a leg back to remove a shadow from the focus of their attention. Stuart moved closer to Laurie and slid his hand into her teddy.

"Not yet," she whispered.

He removed his hand. If not now, when?

They were treated to a potpourri of brightly lit sexual acts performed by and to Ms. Ali, three other women and a host of well-hung men. Whoever was in charge of lighting had a one-track mind—spotlight on the genitals.

123

"I wouldn't mind a few shadows and a softer focus," he whispered.

For the last few minutes, Laurie had been caressing him steadily. Now she leaned into him and whispered, "Touch me."

It was over almost before he knew what had happened. He had been startled to find her wet with desire. She quickly wrapped her legs around his hand and began writhing in a fashion not unlike what was happening on the tube. After finishing in record time, she got down on her hands and knees between his legs and took him with her mouth. Stuart closed his eyes. Paradise Ali, indeed.

Later they lay in bed in the dark, waiting for sleep.

"Why?" he asked.

"Why what?"

"Why did you want to get a movie tonight?"

"I feel like you've gotten bored," she said.

"What about you?"

"I feel it a little, too."

"Maybe it just happens after seven years."

"I'm sure it does," she said. "Would you rather we hadn't gotten the movie?"

"No, I liked it. I felt a little weird, but I liked it."

"I felt weird too. What do you think?"

"It was different. The sort of thing you never think you'll do."

"Maybe that's been one of our problems."

"I didn't think we had any problems."

"Don't get defensive," she said. "It's not a big one."

"Sexual boredom." He sighed. "When do we start using the whips and black-leather masks?"

"If it helped, would you be so against it?"

"I guess I'd just want to put them away when company came."

Claire woke in the middle of the night and cried. Stuart got up and brought her a bottle. While he waited for her to finish it and fall back to sleep, he wandered into the office and stood by the French doors. *She* was there again, perched in the window. He stood in the dark, wondering if she could see him, illuminated only by a few miscast rays of street light. He wondered why he felt disappointed. Sex with Laurie that night had not been significantly different. Maybe it took place in a different atmosphere, maybe she wore different clothes, and they did it in a different part of the house. But the bodies were the same. He loved her and thought she was sexy, but her body held no mystery or surprise for him anymore. All the porno movies in the world would not alter that fact.

She left the window and retreated somewhere into her room. He felt a glimmer of arousal in his groin. Mystery, he thought. Surprise. They hovered out there, just slightly beyond his grasp. To reach them he imagined a tightrope stretched from his window to *hers*. Would he ever have the nerve to walk it? From Claire's room came the sound of a plastic bottle hitting the floor. She'd fallen asleep. Stuart turned away from the doors.

17

LAURIE was packing for the sales conference in Portugal.

"Promise me you won't stay in the house all eight nights with Claire," she said.

"I'm already going out two nights," he said.

"With whom?"

"Thursday and Saturday Eliot and I have nonspecific plans for dinner. I'll get a baby-sitter. And I wouldn't be surprised if he has dinner over here a couple of times too."

"Where's he staying?"

"At his sister's house."

"Did you ask him if he wanted to stay here?"

"I have, but he says he doesn't."

"Why?"

"He says that seeing you will upset him."

Laurie gave him a look.

"It reminds him that he's not home with Carol," Stuart said.

After dinner Thursday night Eliot didn't want to go back to his sister's.

"I can't stand it there," he said, standing on the sidewalk outside La Cantina on Columbus. "She acts like there's been a death in the family. She keeps talking about what a wonderful person Carol was. You'd think she'd died instead of just screwing me over."

Stuart yawned. "Want to stay at my place tonight?"

"Let's go out."

"Can't. I have to work tomorrow."

"Gimme a break, Stu. You work for yourself now, remember? You don't have to do doodly squat if you don't want to."

"Well, then I want to work tomorrow."

Eliot looked up at the streetlight. "Listen to this guy. He can do anything he pleases. His wife's out of town and his best friend is miserable and all he can think about is making a buck."

"I thought you weren't in mourning."

"I'm not. But I'm not exactly in nirvana either. Now come on. Let's just go and have a drink. I know a nice homey place."

Stuart looked at his watch.

"I'll pay for the goddamn baby-sitter," Eliot said.

"It's not that," Stuart said.

"Then what is it?" Eliot asked.

"I don't know exactly," Stuart said.

"That's not good enough," Eliot said. He flagged down a cab.

They wound up at a place in midtown called the Pink Poodle.

"This is a nice homey place?" Stuart asked, standing under the canopy, staring at the large wooden sign proclaiming TOPLESS ENTERTAINMENT.

Eliot grinned. "Sure. Everyone walks around with their clothes off. Just like home."

They walked in, past the bar and into the back, where two naked women were dancing on a platform in the middle of the room. Blue and red lights circled and flashed above them. The air was smoky and smelled slightly of disinfectant. Half the tables and booths around the platform were empty. The other half were filled with Asian men in dark suits.

They sat down in a booth and a waitress in a tight black bathing suit appeared. "Something to drink?"

"Two beers," Eliot said. "In the bottle."

The waitress walked away.

"It's the only way you can be sure of what you're drinking," Eliot said.

"I see you have experience," Stuart said.

"Tell me you never went to a place like this in college," Eliot said.

"I did, but I probably ordered whatever was on tap."

The women on the runway went through their motions monotonously. They looked bored. One was a short, chunky white girl with stringy blond hair, cellulite and small droopy breasts. The other was a tall, good-looking black woman with milk-chocolate skin and lovely round breasts.

"It's proof that in business a black has to be twice as good as a white to qualify for the same job," Eliot said.

Stuart nodded. He had just noticed the television monitors mounted on the wall in each corner of the room. In each monitor his friend Ms. Ali was orally addressing an erect penis.

The waitress in the bathing suit returned with two bottles of Bud. "That'll be twelve dollars."

"Wow," Stuart groaned, reaching for his wallet.

Eliot stopped him. "It's on me."

"You just paid for dinner," Stuart said.

"It's still cheaper than a shrink," Eliot said, putting a twenty on the waitress's tray. To her he said, "I'd really like to see some change from this."

The waitress smirked and left. Eliot picked up his bottle and took a pull.

"I guess glasses are extra," Stuart said.

Eliot slouched down into the booth. They both watched the black woman dance.

"God, she's lovely," Stuart said under his breath.

"Yeah," said Eliot. "Wouldn't mind jumping in the sack with her."

Stuart took a pull on his beer. The black woman winked at him and he smiled back.

"Did I ever tell you about the cocktail waitress at the Neanderthal Hilton?" Eliot asked.

Stuart was finding it difficult to take his eyes off the platform. "Neanderthal?"

"In Cincinnati," Eliot said. "It's actually the Netherlands Hilton, but that's what we called it. This was about three years ago. I was flying in about once a week, working on a convertible bond issue for a fairly good-sized building supply company."

"You were also married at the time."

Eliot shrugged. "Anyway, I'd usually get in around six in the evening and after dinner I'd go down to the cocktail lounge and watch basketball. I remember it was the playoffs so it must have been late April, maybe May. So I start to notice this cocktail waitress. Really cute, terrific boobs, tiny hands and feet, a little pageboy haircut. One night I said something about her hands and she told me she used to model rings, gloves and shoes for catalogues. She even showed me some photos.

"So it becomes pretty obvious after a few trips that we're getting friendly. Don't ask me why. Maybe she's impressed because I'm from New York and I wear a nice suit. And I sort of enjoy her. I mean, she's from Covington, which is Kentucky side of life and sort of slummy, but she's bright and funny. Understand that her idea of a big night out is chili at the Skyline and the road show of *Cats*. I also start to tip pretty nice once I realize that I might have a shot at jumping her."

Stuart took another pull from his beer. He was finishing it quickly. "I can't believe she could be any nicer than what you had at home."

"Variety, Stu." Eliot finished his beer and motioned the waitress for two more. "Anyway, this goes on for a month.

I mean, a couple of times I hint about getting together after work, but she ignores me. So I figure she's just a tease. Or maybe she thinks she can pump me for good tips, in which case she's right."

The new beers arrived. Stuart hadn't finished his first yet.

"Except it's starting to drive me nuts," Eliot said. "I mean, I go to bed dreaming about her. I even start fantasizing about her while I'm making love to Carol."

"Talk about overkill," Stuart said. He'd caught the black woman's eye again. She was smiling at him, licking her lips. Almost in spite of himself, he felt stimulated.

"So it really starts to get to me, being jerked around like that with my tongue hanging out," Eliot said. "I finally decide I've had enough and I'm going to start staying at the Westin. Except I'm going to tell her first. So the next time I get to the Neanderthal I go down for a drink like usual. She comes over and says hello and we start kidding around and teasing just like every other time. Except after a while I happen to mention that my company has made a deal with Westin and now all their employees have to stay there. I mean it's total bullshit, but she swallows it. And all of a sudden she looks like the world has caved in, like she's going to cry. I couldn't believe it."

Stuart cleared his throat. "Did you ever happen to mention that you were married?"

Eliot shrugged. "What do you think?" Before he could continue, a skinny brunette in a bathing suit came over and sat down in the booth with them. "Buy me a drink, honey?"

"Forget it, babe," Eliot said. "I'm talking to my friend."

The woman stood up and put a red helium balloon attached to a small wooden anchor on their table.

"What is the significance of this?" Stuart asked, poking the balloon.

"It means we're not available to be hustled," Eliot said. "Anyway, where was I?"

"She was about to cry."

"Oh, yeah, right. I mean, I don't know, maybe she thought we were participating in some strange Cincinnati mating ritual or something. Anyway, she's so upset that she actually arranges to get off work and insists that we go up to my room to talk about it. And you know what?"

Stuart shook his head. The black woman was rubbing her body with her hands. On the wall monitors, Ms. Ali was lying on her back while another woman sampled her wares. Stuart realized his palms were damp.

"I thought she really wanted to talk," Eliot said. "I mean, on the way up to my room I'm trying to figure out how to explain the Westin thing. Then the next thing I know we get inside the door and she grabs me."

Eliot paused for a moment. He must have noticed that the black woman had moved to the corner of the platform closest to them and was watching Stuart as she bent back, limbo fashion.

"What is this?" he whispered.

"Nothing," Stuart said. "You got into your room and she grabbed you."

Eliot glanced from the black woman to him. "Yeah, so the next thing I know, we're in bed. She's in her panties and I'm in my shorts. And all of a sudden the game starts all over again. She turns her back to me and I slide my arms around her and caress her breasts. I'm kissing her neck, ears and shoulders, trying to turn her around but she won't face me. I mean, I don't know what's going on inside her head, but I've got an erection like the goddamn Sears Tower. Sometimes I get her twisted halfway around and she gives me some tongue, but every time my hands go below her waist, she stops me."

Stuart felt a light sweat break out on his forehead. Somehow his second beer was already empty and he himself was signaling the waitress for a third. And talk about the Sears Tower. On the platform the black woman had started touching her breasts, circling the dark aureoles with the tips of her fingers.

131

"You can't believe how long this went on," Eliot said. "I mean, practically the whole night. You know what it's like to have an erection for six straight hours? It's a hard-on marathon. About four o'clock in the morning I'm on heartbreak hill. I mean I can't get in and I can't let go and I keep thinking that I have a goddamn breakfast meeting with the chief financial officer in four hours."

"Did you talk?" Stuart asked.

"Sure we talked. She told me that she was once married to a guy who used to sit in an empty bathtub, reading *Penthouse* and playing with himself. The guy must have been out of his mind. Unless she did to him every night what she was doing to me, in which case it was perfectly understandable."

The next set of beers arrived and Stuart quickly took a gulp. He felt light-headed, almost giddy.

"Anyway," Eliot said. "The next thing I know, it's starting to get light out. I must have dozed off or something. But I wake up and she's turned around in bed, watching me. I mean, by now I'm totally disoriented and exhausted but believe it or not, I've still got a hard-on.

"So like the room is filled with this dim gray dawn light and I'm still not sure whether this is a dream or not. Except there's this little smile on her lips and she says, 'Okay.' Like in her mind I passed some kind of test. And the next thing I know she pushes me over on my back and pulls my shorts off. I can't believe this is going on, Stu. It's like I already gave up and surrendered and now they're telling me the judges made a mistake and I'm the winner after all. She's going down on me and her breasts are bouncing on my thighs and I'm thinking to myself that if there was ever a moment in my life where I'd like to become frozen in time forever, this is it. Except I'm wrong because next she slips off her panties and climbs on top of me."

Stuart was starting to feel dizzy. He knew it wasn't just the beer. It was Eliot's Ph.D. dissertation in erotica and the black woman who was smiling dreamily at him and sliding her middle finger up the inside of her naked thigh and over the bushy mound of black hair between her legs.

"And Stuart, this was the single most erotic moment of my life," Eliot said. "She plants her hands on my shoulders and begins to move. Slowly. Just her hips. Tucking them up, grinding them against me. I've got my face in her tits and my hands on her ass and each time she slides up against me I feel this tingling wave of pure sexual pleasure like nothing I have ever felt in my life."

The black woman squatted on the platform in front of Stuart and licked her lips slowly. Their eyes were fixed on each other. Her legs opened and she reached down between them and parted herself with her fingers. Stuart's heart was beating wildly. His jockey shorts felt three sizes too small. He wanted to throw himself at her feet, crawl on his hands and his knees and press his face into her.

The black woman brought her fingers to her lips.

"*I give up!*" Stuart shouted. The next thing he knew, he was on his feet, staring at her, breathing hard, his heart thumping.

"Hey, Stu . . ." Eliot reached for his arm. Stuart's eyes met the black woman's. Her legs snapped shut.

Eliot shook him. "Stu?"

The black woman backed away. Stuart felt dizzy. Sweat broke out on his forehead. He was aware that the Asian men were staring at him, grinning and murmuring to each other. He turned to them. "I, uh, meant I have to call the baby-sitter."

Eliot started to laugh. "Let's just go," he gasped.

A few minutes later they were in a cab, heading uptown. Eliot was still laughing. Stuart grinned, but he was horribly embarrassed. For a split second back in the Pink Poodle he'd been out of control. As if a dark force inside had taken over.

"I really thought you were gonna jump on that stage," Eliot said, wiping tears out of his eyes. "And then you told everyone you had to call the fucking baby-sitter!"

The cabby looked in the rearview mirror and grinned.

"I don't know what happened," Stuart said. "I guess I just went over the limit."

"'I give up!' he yells," Eliot said. "'I give up!'"

"Okay, cut it out," Stuart said.

"Stu 'I give up!' Miller," Eliot said.

"I said cut it out."

It took Eliot a moment to calm down.

"So what was the end of the story?" Stuart asked as they turned up West End.

"The Neanderthal girl? She left the next morning while I was in the shower. The next time I went to Cincinnati, I stayed at the Westin."

The cab stopped in front of Stuart's building. "That's it?"

"Incredible, huh?" Eliot yawned.

"I don't know. I can't figure out why you told me."

"You serious?" Eliot stared at him from the other side of the cab seat.

Stuart nodded.

"Cause I don't want you to think that she dumped me totally, birdbrain."

"Carol?"

"Jesus Christ," Eliot muttered. "Who else?"

18

LAURIE sounded distant, which was understandable since she was calling from Portugal.

"How's it going?" Stuart asked.

"Okay."

"How's Portugal?"

"It's nice."

"How're the sale meetings?"

"Okay."

"Anything you want to tell me?"

"The weather's been beautiful. The conference is crazy. That's all. Can I speak to Claire?"

"Hold on." He got Claire and sat her in his lap, holding the phone next to her ear.

"Okay, she's on," he said.

"Claire, can you hear me?" Laurie asked.

"Yes."

"This is Mommy."

"Mommy . . . airpane."

"That's right. Mommy took an airplane. She went to Portugal."

"Airpane . . . Mommy."

"Does Claire miss Mommy?"

"Airpane . . . Mommy." Claire started to squirm off his lap.

"Claire, baby, do you miss your mommy?" Laurie asked from three thousand miles away. But Claire had wiggled down onto the floor to look at Stuart's computer printer.

"She wouldn't stay on the phone," Stuart said.

"Okay, I'll call again in a couple of days," Laurie said. Stuart sensed that she was about to hang up. "Wait."

"What?"

"I miss you. Do you love me?"

"Yes, of course I do."

"Okay. Well, take care."

"I will, Woof. Bye."

The weekend arrived. Stuart put Claire in the car and took her up to his parents' house in Harrison. He parked in the driveway and his mother opened the front door and waved. She was wearing a yellow blouse and a pair of denim slacks with an elastic waist. She looked very thin and more wrinkled than a healthy woman in her early sixties (she was three years older than his father) should have been. Stuart thought she would have looked better if she'd dyed her hair instead of letting it go all gray. With some auburn in her hair she'd look like Katharine Hepburn.

"Gramma, gramma!" Claire shrieked as Stuart tried to release her from the car seat. It had as many belts and straps as an electric chair. Finally he freed her and she ran up the slate walk and into Grandma's arms.

Stuart followed behind, carrying two *Sesame Street* canvas bags full of support materials—diapers, wipes, books, balls, toys and Cheerios.

"Where's Dad?" He asked as he stepped into the house. It felt cool inside, but not air-conditioned.

His mother didn't seem to hear him. She was busy coddling Claire. "How's my little girl?"

"Mom?" Stuart said.

"He's at the club."

"When's he coming home?"

"Does Claire want a cookie?"

"Cookie, cookie." Claire squirmed out of her arms to the floor and ran into the kitchen. Grandma followed.

"Mom . . ."

"I don't know, darling, you'll have to speak to him."

"When was the last time *you* spoke to him?"

"I don't recall."

He left Claire with Grandma and drove up to the club. The sky was bright blue and dotted with cotton-puff clouds. Not much breeze; good golf weather. His father was sitting alone at a glass table under an umbrella on the slate terrace in front of the main clubhouse. Across the driveway to his left was the eighteenth hole. Down the hill to his right was the pool. He was eating lunch.

"Hello, Stuart!"

Stuart sat down. "I was hoping we'd all have lunch at home," he said.

His father took a bite of his turkey club sandwich. "Can't. She threw me out."

"What do you mean, she threw you out?"

"She told me to leave and not come back."

"Dad, it's just as much your house as hers."

"I won't go where I'm not wanted."

"Great, so where are you staying?"

"I've got a place."

"What kind of place?"

"It's comfortable. That's all I need."

"I can't believe this. I thought you said she couldn't live without you."

"Maybe I was wrong."

A florid-faced man with a broad belly, wearing a hot-pink polo shirt and pastel plaid slacks came up to the table. "Hello, Stuart."

Stuart stood up and shook his meaty hand. "Hello, Mr. Werner."

"How's the wife and little one?"

"Fine." I'm thirty-four years old, Stuart thought. Why am I still addressing this man by his surname?

"I hear you're a real hotshot at Bingham."

"I left."

"No kidding? Got a better offer?"

"Went on my own."

Werner clubbed him on the shoulder. "That's the spirit!" He turned to Stuart's father. "Ready to get your butt hauled?"

"By who?"

"Five dollars a hole. Match play."

"I hope you brought cash," Mr. Miller said, dabbing his lips with his napkin.

"Meet you at one in ten minutes." Werner turned to Stuart. "Think you can support this bum in his old age?"

"If it comes to that."

"Oh, it will," Werner said, with a laugh. "Believe me, the way he plays it will."

Stuart's father watched Werner waddle away. "Son of a bitch plays out of an eighteen when he should be a fourteen."

"Then why do you play him?"

"Makes it interesting."

"Dad, what the hell is going on at home?"

"I told you, she threw me out."

"Why?"

His father shrugged. "Ask her."

He drove back to the house. Grandma was weeding the flower beds in front, down on her knees with a weeding tool and a brown paper bag from the supermarket. Claire was sitting in the sun, playing with some leaves.

"She probably needs sun block, Mom," Stuart said.

"No," said Claire. "No bock."

Stuart went into the house and got the number-fifteen sun screen from one of the *Sesame Street* bags.

Claire eyed him warily when he returned. Stuart kneeled down next to her and squirted the white lotion into his hand, then started to spread it on her shoulders and arms.

"No bock!" Claire shrieked, trying to twist out of his grip. Stuart held her tightly and managed to apply it to her arms, face and neck.

"You used to get so tan in the summer," his mother said. "We never put suntan lotion on you. We just let you turn red, then brown."

"She'll be back in the city tomorrow, turning red then white," Stuart said.

"It's a terrible place to bring up a child."

"We're making the best of it."

"Your wife won't move to the suburbs?"

"Her name's Laurie, Mom."

"You said she went to Spain on business?"

"Portugal."

"What kind of business does she have there?"

"It's a sales conference."

His mother set her jaw. "Your father used to go to sales conferences."

"I guess that says it all, huh?" Stuart asked.

Claire jumped up and pointed down. "Bug."

Stuart looked at the ground. A ladybug was clinging to a blade of grass. "It's a ladybug."

"Lay bee bug."

"Here." Stuart pulled the blade of grass up and held it for her to see.

Claire backed away. "Lay bee bug."

"Dee. Lay . . . dee. Put your tongue against the roof of your mouth and go *dee*."

"Bee. Lay . . . bee."

"She speaks well for a child her age," his mother said, getting up slowly and stiffly. She picked up the brown bag.

"Let me carry it, Mom."

"A bag of weeds? I can manage."

"I was only trying to help." Stuart took Claire's hand and they walked with Grandma to the garage. "I saw Dad at the club. He said you'd thrown him out."

"He's chosen his own course."

"Would you mind telling me what this is all about?"

"He has to grow up, Stuart."

"He's sixty."

"He was always immature." In the garage she dropped the bag into one of the plastic garbage pails, replaced the weeding tool on the pegboard rack and removed her gardening gloves. "What would you like for lunch?"

"Whatever."

"And Claire?"

"Whatever cut into small pieces."

Claire ate well. She had tuna fish, sliced tomatoes and celery. Stuart could not recall seeing her eat so much in a single sitting.

"It must be the fresh suburban air," he said, and quickly regretted it.

"If you moved out here you could have fresh air all the time."

"Maybe when Claire's a little older."

"Are you thinking about having another one?"

"I don't know, Mom. They're kind of expensive."

"That's not a good reason."

A devious thought occurred to him. "How come you never had more, Mom?"

"I couldn't."

"Couldn't?"

"The doctors never understood why. Of course your father refused to be tested."

"I guess he figured he'd already passed," Stuart said.

"So had I," said his mother.

Claire's eyes started to roll up into her head. Stuart picked her up.

140

"Want to put her on the bed upstairs?" his mother whispered.

"I'd rather put her on something on the floor so she doesn't roll off."

His mother left and returned with a down comforter, which she laid in a corner of the living room near the kitchen door. Stuart put Claire down on it. She was already asleep.

They went back into the kitchen and his mother made herself a cup of coffee.

"Want to tell me what the story with Dad is?" Stuart asked.

"He can come back when he learns to behave like a human being."

"Can you get more specific?"

"No."

Back at the club, he found his father teeing off at the sixth hole with Werner. His father's drive pulled to the left but caught the edge of the fairway. Werner's drive sliced to the right and disappeared into the rough.

"I'm in jail," Werner said.

"You take the cart," Stuart's father told him, taking a five iron and a wedge. "We'll walk."

He and Stuart set out down the fairway.

"How're you doing?" Stuart asked.

"I'm down two holes, but he's out of it here. So I'll be down one. Just keep an eye on him so he doesn't cheat."

Stuart glanced back toward Werner, who'd gotten out of the cart and was wandering around the trees on the other side of the fairway.

"I blew a two-footer on three," his father said.

"Dad, I'm getting tired of asking this, but what's going on?"

"With your mother?"

"Jesus Christ, Dad, who else?"

"Stuart, just because a man reaches sixty it doesn't mean he looses his dignity."

"I know that, Dad."

"Well, apparently your mother doesn't."

"Look, Dad, this isn't an easy question for me to ask, but are you telling me that Mom won't have sex with you anymore?"

"Sex? Who said anything about sex?"

"Then what is it?"

"It's complicated." His father found his ball in the rough and selected the five iron.

"What's so complicated?" Stuart asked, exasperated.

"Shh." Mr. Miller took a practice swing, ripping a wet green swath through the grass. Then he took a small step forward and readied himself over his ball. He brought the iron back and swung. The ball blasted out and sailed up over the fairway toward the green.

"Good shot, Dad."

His father smiled broadly, then looked across the fairway in time to see Werner whack his ball up into a tree and have it fall back down practically at his feet.

"Fine, wonderful."

They started walking toward the green.

"What is it, Dad?"

"What?"

"That's so complicated with Mom?"

Mr. Miller stopped in the middle of the fairway to watch Werner swing again. This time the ball took off in a line drive and landed in a sand trap just short of the green. His father smiled and started walking again.

"Why is this so important to you, Stuart?"

"Because I'd like to see the two of you get along."

"Why?"

"Why? Because it's very unnerving when your parents aren't getting along. And because it's obvious that neither of you is happy. I'd like to see you happy."

"That's an admirable way for a son to feel."

"So what's the story?"

"Your mother and I do not see eye to eye."

"No kidding."

"That's the story."

"Dad, what is it that you're so angry about? What is it that you resent so much?"

His father looked at him and took a deep breath. "I resent spending my life being made a fool of. I resent spending a life being rebuffed for what I naturally deserved. And I resent the fact that on those rare occasions when she did treat me well, she always made damn sure I knew she was doing me a favor. You get to a point in life, Stuart, where you realize that all you want is someone who's happy to be with you."

"So you start having affairs and you get kicked out of the house."

His father didn't answer. They'd reached the bunkers. Werner had gone ahead in the cart and was now down in the sand trap with a wedge. He blasted the ball out and onto the green and then turned to Stuart's father.

"Three on."

"Four. I saw you hit it twice under that tree."

"Oh, right."

Stuart watched his father two-putt to win the hole. The tee for the seventh was a long walk or a short trip in the cart. Stuart took his father aside. Werner waited in the cart.

"I'm not going to follow you around the course. Is there someplace I can call you tonight?"

"Call me here."

"The club?"

"The card room." There was a small room off the men's locker room where cards were played.

"How late?"

"As late as you want."

"*That's* where you're staying?"

Werner cleared his throat and nodded down the fairway.

A foursome was standing about one hundred sixty yards away, waiting for them to clear the green.

His father got into the cart. "Give Claire a big kiss for me. Talk to you later."

Claire was awake when he got back to the house. She was sitting in Grandma's lap and they were paging through an old photo album. Stuart recognized it at once: his baby pictures.

"Daddy! Daddy!" Claire hopped off Grandma's lap and ran to him. He scooped her up and brought her back to the couch.

"Having fun?"

"We were just looking at pictures of you when you were a baby."

"Baby Daddy, baby Daddy."

"How long has Dad been living in the club locker room?" Stuart asked.

"Is that what he told you?"

"He said I could call him there anytime tonight."

"You were so cute as a baby," his mother said.

"Mom . . ."

"He can live anyplace he wants as far as I'm concerned."

"This is ridiculous."

His mother closed the album. "No, Stuart, this is life."

19

STUART left before dinner. He couldn't deal with his parents' cryptic riddles. Claire fell asleep in the car and woke up cranky. When they got back to the city she insisted that Stuart carry her into the building, so he cradled her in one arm and carried the two *Sesame Street* bags in the other. He let himself in the apartment and found the telephone ringing. Still holding Claire, he answered it.

"Want to get something to eat?" It was Eliot.

"Yeah, but I have to warn you, I've got Claire."

"It's cool. I could use some female companionship."

"How do you feel about Burger King?"

"A great place for a first date."

Stuart put Claire in the stroller and pushed her toward Broadway. He hated Burger King, but it was the easiest place to take Claire.

"King, King!" Claire squealed as they neared the familiar orange and red sign. "Fench fies, fench fies!"

Eliot was waiting for them. They went inside and Stuart put Claire in a plastic high chair and bought her a large order of fries. He got himself something purportedly composed of chicken. Eliot got a Whopper, large fries and a Coke. They found a table next to an old woman who mumbled to herself while she dipped a tea bag in a Styrofoam cup.

"So what did you do today?" Stuart asked Eliot.

"I sat in Riverside Park for a while," he said.

"Where?" Stuart asked.

"On a bench across from the apartment."

"Spying?"

Eliot looked down at his Whopper. "More like crying."

"Serious?"

He nodded. "I was okay in the morning. ESPN had women's volleyball. You'd be amazed. It's not bad. But then they went to this stupid hovercraft racing and it just bored the shit out of me. So I took a walk and the next thing I knew I was sitting on a bench looking up at the apartment."

"Have you talked to her?"

"What's to talk about? She's screwing another man. She says she's in love with him. It's over."

"Maybe she'll change her mind."

"Oh, yeah, great. Just what I want. Good old Eliot, always there for her to come back to between humps."

"Humpy Dumpy," said Claire.

Stuart smiled at her.

"I think I will call her, though. Just to let her know I'm putting the place on the market."

"What's the rush?" Stuart asked.

"It's half mine. Why should she live there while I sleep on my sister's floor?"

"Then tell her to move out."

Eliot shrugged. "The hell with it. I couldn't live there anyway. Too many bad memories."

The old lady next to them was still dipping her tea bag in the cup. Both Stuart and Eliot seemed to notice at the same time.

146

"Maybe she sits there and does it all day," Eliot said in a low voice. "She reads the leaves. Burger King's resident fortune teller. There's a Whopper in your future. By the way, did you hear what Jesus told the Polish people just before he was crucified?"

Stuart shook his head.

"He took them aside and said, 'Listen, you guys, play dumb till I get back.'"

Stuart didn't laugh.

"What's with you?" Eliot asked.

"My mother threw my father out of the house. He's living in the card room in the men's locker at the club."

"Is there any extra space? Maybe I could move in with him."

"I can't believe you and he are going through this at the same time," Stuart said.

Eliot gasped. "Your mom's porking some other guy?"

"I doubt it," Stuart said. "But why is it that the husbands always seem to be the ones who are thrown out?"

"I always thought it was because they had someplace else to go," Eliot said. "Obviously I've begun to wonder about that myself lately. Does your old man have a girlfriend?"

"I don't know."

"Then what's the problem?"

"I can't tell. It's a big secret they won't talk about. All I know is my mother says he can come home when he starts acting like a human being again."

Eliot grinned. "That could be a lot to ask."

Stuart was not amused.

"Okay, okay. I know it must be upsetting."

"They're in their sixties," Stuart said. "You'd think they might want to start enjoying each other for a change."

"The number of divorces among people over fifty is rising faster than any other age group."

"Where'd you hear that?"

"The *Ladies' Home Journal*."

"You read . . ."

"Listen, when you're trying to figure out why your marriage is falling apart you'll read anything."

After dinner Eliot went to a movie. Stuart stopped at the Video Connection and rented *Charlotte's Web* for Claire. At home he made them popcorn. They watched the movie one and a half times and then Claire fell asleep. Stuart put her in bed and closed the door.

The apartment felt empty without Laurie. He wandered into the kitchen, but wasn't hungry. Next he turned on the TV and spun through the channels but nothing interesting caught his eye. Why did every moment in life either have to be entertaining or a step toward future success?

He went into his office. It was ten P.M. on a Saturday night. He could read the half dozen annual reports lying on his desk, or some investor newsletters, or flip on one of his terminals and check what was happening in whatever part of the world still had open markets.

Or he could turn off the lights and go over to the French doors and see what was going on across the street. Which is what he did.

Most of the windows in the Excelsior Arms were covered with shades. In one that wasn't, a man wearing jockey shorts was dancing vigorously by himself. In another, three men were sitting at a table, drinking and talking. *Her* shade was drawn, the light on behind it. He could see her shadow against the shade. Then the shadow of someone taller. Both of them passing back and forth rapidly. It seemed they were dressing. Probably getting ready to go out. But where? And to do what? He wished he could follow them. Wished he could see how the other half of the street lived. Laurie said having a child meant the loss of spontaneity. You couldn't just drop everything and run out anymore. Suppose they'd never had Claire. Would he really have followed *her*?

The intercom buzzed.

"Mr. Berger," the doorman said.

"Let him up."

Stuart waited at the door for him. "That was fast."

Eliot looked glum. "Nothing more depressing than going to a movie alone."

"People do it all the time," Stuart said.

"People who don't have anyone else to go to the movies with," Eliot said. He looked down at the floor. "Jesus, I can't believe this is happening to me." Then he looked back at Stuart. "Let's get drunk."

"I'll have a drink with you."

"I can't even find someone to get drunk with?"

"Don't get maudlin. What if Claire wakes up?"

"She doesn't know what drunk is," Eliot said.

"I wouldn't want her to see me intoxicated."

"Okay," Eliot said. "Where's the liquor?"

Eliot made a martini. Stuart had a gin and tonic that was mostly tonic. He simply wasn't in the mood to drink. They sat down in front of the television set and turned on ESPN. Baseball. Boston was playing the Angels.

"Thank God for sports," Eliot said, taking a gulp of his drink. "Thank God for Boston."

"Eliot, what's happening to you?" Stuart asked.

Eliot scowled. "What?"

"You said before that you can't believe this was happening to you."

"Carol, dummy."

"Think you can answer a question just once without insulting me?" Stuart asked.

"Hey, I'm sorry, man," Eliot said. "I guess I'm just pissed."

Stuart nodded. He was willing to let it go. They stared at the television for a while.

"You know what's funny?" Eliot said. "In a way it's a relief. I never thought Carol would stay with me. It's like I spent our entire marriage waiting for this to happen. Now I don't have to worry about whether she's sleeping with anyone because I know."

"Why didn't you think Carol would stay with you?"

Eliot smirked at him. "You're a good friend, Stuart, but if insight could be measured optically, you'd be blind. I mean, look at that woman. She's a goddess. What does she need a wimp like me for? I knew she'd figure it out someday. It's like the Dorothy Stratton story. You know, *Star 80*. Small-time hustler finds this beautiful girl in a Tastee-Freez out in the sticks of Saskatchewan or someplace and brings her to Hollywood. At first she thinks he's the greatest thing in the world, but then she starts to meet directors and film stars and *poof,* she's gone."

"You're not a small-time hustler."

"It's all relative," Eliot said. "I don't know anything about this guy she's banging, but I can promise you this. He either looks like Adonis or he's rolling in megabucks. You'll see."

"How will I see?"

"Because when I cut his balls off there'll be a picture of him in the papers. Aw, shit!"

On the TV one of the Boston players had just struck out with bases loaded and two outs. Stuart stared at Eliot. "Sometimes you worry me."

Eliot stared at the replay. "Sometimes I worry myself."

20

LAURIE returned from Portugal tanned and depressed.
"What's wrong?" Stuart asked.
She shrugged. "Nothing."
"Didn't have a good time?"
"I had a great time."
"So?"
"So it's just hard to come back, that's all."
"To me?"
"No, not you."
"Claire?"
"No, of course not. But I'll tell you something funny. I really didn't miss her as much as I thought I would. I just didn't think about her, except when I saw another little child."
"Then what is it? Your job?"
"No, my job's fine. Everything's fine and I'm happy to be back."
"But . . ."
"I don't know. Everything's the same. It was so different in Portugal. Coming back just makes it all seem worse."

About a week later a thick envelope full of snapshots arrived in the mail. Laurie had taken the disk camera to Portugal. Although it was addressed to her, he opened the envelope.

"Who were those guys?" he asked after dinner. Laurie was sitting on the couch, reading a book to Claire.

"What guys?"

"The guys in the pictures from Portugal."

"Let me see."

He brought her the pictures and sat down next to Claire.

"Piktahs, piktahs!"

Laurie sifted through the photos—shots of a modern-looking seaside resort, the beach, the interior of her room. Groups of men and women in bathing suits.

"Beach, beach." Claire pointed at a photo.

"That's where Mommy was," Laurie told her.

"Airpane, airpane."

"She took a plane to the beach."

"Fahway, fahway."

"The beach in Portugal was faraway."

"There, that one," Stuart said.

Laurie held up a photo of her seated between two men at an outdoor table covered with drinks. The man on her left was paunchy and balding with pale white skin. The man on her right was wiry and darkly tanned with short black curly hair and a mustache. Laurie was wearing a purple bathing suit and had a dreamy smile which made Stuart think she was a little drunk.

"That's Ed Barkley, head of US sales, and Ramone, who works in the European office."

"Looks like you got pretty chummy."

"We did." She thumbed through a few more shots, passing one of Ramone on the beach wearing a tiny black bikini bathing suit.

"Why didn't he just go nude?"

"You'll have to ask him," she said.

"Who's that?" he asked when she got to a photo of a shapely woman wrapped in a bath towel and wearing a large straw hat.

"That was my roommate, Suzy. She's in sales."

"You had to share a room?"

"Everyone did, but I didn't see much of her. She spent most of the nights at Ed's."

"Ed, head of US sales?"

She nodded.

"Married?"

She nodded again.

"And Suzy?"

"Not married."

"And, uh, where did Ed's roommate spend his time?"

Laurie shrugged.

"You don't know or you won't tell me," Stuart said.

"What do you think?" she asked.

"There's nothing wrong with a little harmless flirting," Laurie said later. It was dark. They were in bed, almost asleep. He wondered why she always waited until he was just falling off to start a serious conversation.

"What does harmless flirting mean?"

"It means exactly what it sounds like."

He opened his eyes and stared up into the dark. "Does it include unmarried Suzy spending the night with married Ed?"

"God, Stuart, do I even have to answer that?"

"Who did you harmlessly flirt with?"

"The other one mostly, Ramone."

"The one with the microscopic bathing suit."

"He was extremely charming. It was fun."

"Fun?"

"European men are different."

"Let me guess. Inside that bathing suit was a bologna sandwich."

"More refined and elegant."

153

He pushed himself up onto his elbows and leaned back against the headboard. "Are you sure you want to tell me this?"

"Haven't you ever had a crush?"

"Wait a minute. How did we get from harmless flirting to having a crush?"

"It's all the same."

"But different from sleeping with someone."

"Markedly."

"How about feeling someone up?"

"That's crude, Stuart."

"Three weeks ago we made love while watching a porno movie and now I'm being crude."

"In this context."

"So how did you leave it?"

"Leave what?"

"Leave the harmlessly flirtatious, nearly naked Ramone, object of your crush? Same time next year's sale conference?"

"He's coming here in October."

"You two just can't stand to be apart, huh?"

"On business. And I don't like your snotty tone. I've told him all about you. I was hoping the three of us would go out to dinner."

"And maybe catch a porno flick afterward?"

Laurie rolled over, presenting him with her back. "You're impossible."

"I'm impossible? You're off having crushes and harmlessly flirting with some porno star named Ramone while I stay at home and watch Claire for eight straight days and I'm supposed to be thrilled for you?"

"Shhh, you'll wake her."

"So? Claire wakes me at least once a night. Why can't I wake her sometimes?"

"Go ahead, wake her."

"I don't understand why you told me."

"I didn't think you'd react this way. Haven't you ever had a crush?"

"I work alone all day. Who am I going to have a crush on, the mailman?"

"Well, if you did you'd understand."

"I'm sorry. He's not my type."

Laurie said nothing. He looked at the clock. It was nearly one A.M.

"Why do you always wait until the middle of the night to have these conversations?" he asked. "Now I'm wide awake wondering if my wife has been, is being now, or plans to be unfaithful to me."

"Can *you* swear that you'll be faithful for the rest of your life?" she asked.

"I have no plans otherwise."

"Neither do I."

21

$S$$HE$ was lackadaisical about keeping the shade down. It was always down in the morning while she slept, but she would often open it after she awoke. Then, it was as before—she would lean out, her naked breasts swaying in the sunlight. He would stand by the French doors and watch. He was certain now that she knew he was there. When they were both at their windows they played a little game of pretending not to notice each other.

He decided he wanted to meet her, to talk to her. If Laurie could have a crush, he could at least satisfy his curiosity about *her* life. Where did she go every night? What did she do? If she knew he watched her, why did she continue to parade in front of the window in the nude?

Staring at Lockheed options on the Quotron, he imagined taking her someplace nice for lunch. A restaurant with cream-colored tablecloths, fresh flowers, and crystal. She would be wearing a black dress, with a black hat and veil. Her manner would be reserved, but he'd find he could make her laugh. Before dessert he would kiss her hand. After lunch they'd take a cab to the Helmsley Palace or one of the other midtown hotels, and abandon themselves to the growing lust they felt for each other. Later she would refuse to take a taxi home with him, concerned that at rush hour someone he knew might see them together. She would not call. She would wait to hear from him.

Stuart sat back and stretched, amused at his overactive imagination. But he did want to meet her. The question was, How? He didn't know her name or room number and he couldn't just sit in the lobby of the hotel waiting for her. How would he introduce himself? *"Hi, I'm the guy who watches you parade around your room naked."* Somehow it didn't have the right ring to it.

He decided his best chance was in the evening when she went out. By altering his route home from the IFIL slightly, he could push Claire down the block past the hotel. Sooner or later he would run into her.

The idea appealed to him for another reason—she would see him with Claire. If he stopped and introduced himself, Claire would act as a buffer, a shock absorber. Obviously, he couldn't have anything immediately carnal on his mind when he had his two-year-old daughter with him. He could explain who he was and add that since they looked at each other all the time, he thought they might as well get introduced. He wouldn't say anything about seeing her naked. He'd just ask if she might want to have lunch sometime. Or maybe just a cup of coffee. She could pick the place. He'd even bring Claire along if she liked.

For the next week he took the new route home. Each day he slowed down as he approached her block until he and the stroller were moving at a snail's pace.

"Slow down. Slow down," Claire said one day as they turned the corner.

"That's right, Claire."

"Tree, time for tree."

An elm grew out of the sidewalk near the hotel and Stuart had taken to stopping the stroller near it. Then he would pretend to have a botanical interest while waiting to see if *she* emerged.

She didn't.

He began to realize that the chances of meeting her on the sidewalk were not as good as he had originally thought. He could not spend more than a few minutes outside the hotel without feeling conspicuous. He started to see the same faces. Might they be wondering what he was doing there? After all, how interesting could a tree be?

A summer storm blew in one afternoon, bringing thunder and showers, then sprinkles, then moments of no rain at all. Stuart stood at the French doors, watching her window and speaking to Eliot on the phone.

"You should have seen the girl I went out with last night."

"What are you talking about?" Stuart asked.

"One of the secretaries in the office set me up."

"They know about you and Carol?"

"Half my office takes the Lex line every morning," Eliot said. "They see me coming from my sister's. I figured I'd rather they knew the truth than let the rumors fly."

"So you told them?"

"I told them we were separated."

"And someone set you up?"

"Sure, why not? I don't want them to think I'm sitting at home playing with myself. This was my second blind date. I had one on Monday, too."

"How did that one go?"

"Just great. I developed a special attraction for her."

"Really?"

"Yeah, it's called gravity. She must have weighed three hundred pounds."

"Ha ha."

"So let me tell you about this girl last night," Eliot said. "She was twenty-one. A nursing student with a body that would make Hugh Hefner drool. I take her to the Surf Club. Twenty bucks a head at the door. She says it's too much, we should go to a movie instead. I just laugh. Inside she says she'll just have club soda because the drinks are five bucks. I mean, she can't believe that this is a blind date and I'm gonna drop a hundred on her."

"Maybe she was worried about what you'd expect later," Stuart said.

"Maybe, but she had two fuzzy navels and then she didn't seem too worried about anything."

"So?"

"So she lives in a women's dorm and I'm staying at my sister's."

"You mean, that was it?"

"Almost."

"Almost?"

"We had a make-out session outside the dorm. I felt like I was in high school again. Lots of tongue action and some under-the-blouse, over-the-bra stuff."

"Will you see her again?"

"I doubt it."

"Why not? It sounds like you liked each other."

"Jesus, Stu, she's a nursing student. A kid. Her idea of a big time is pizza and a movie."

"So?"

"So I want to marry a woman who's got some class. A sense of style. Carol had style."

"Eliot, you're not even divorced yet. How can you talk about getting married again? Maybe you'd enjoy going out with some women."

"The hell with that. I just want it the way it used to be. If not with Carol, then with someone else. I can't deal with all this dating bullshit again."

159

Across the street *she* left the hotel holding a black umbrella and pulling a handcart containing a blue laundry bag.

"I've got to go," Stuart said.

"What is it?"

"Something hot just came across the screen," he lied.

"Want to share it?"

"Uh . . ."

"Okay, I know you like to play it close to the vest. Go get 'em, tiger."

It was drizzling lightly and he had not bothered to take a jacket or umbrella. As he walked up the sidewalk toward Broadway, he imagined the scene. She would be sitting in the laundromat reading a magazine. He would walk in and sit down next to her. She would give him a funny look because he hadn't brought any laundry. He would explain who he was and they would take it from there.

He turned right on Broadway and walked toward the closest laundromat. Because of the rain, the sidewalks were not crowded.

He stopped outside the laundromat and looked through the glass. Just as he'd imagined, she was there. The discovery actually startled him. In her room across the street she was more fantasy than reality, but here, just a few feet away, she was suddenly living, breathing, doing laundry.

Stuart stood outside uncertain how to proceed. All of a sudden, the idea of just walking in didn't appeal to him. Inside it was dingy and cramped. A row of washing machines lined one wall, a row of driers lined the other, and a flat wooden bench ran down the middle. Sitting on the bench, wearing black slacks and a tight yellow sleeveless top, her black hair pulled into a thick braid behind her head, *she* was staring at the washing machine in front of her. Not far from her a tall, lanky guy wearing blue jeans and cowboy boots sat reading the newspaper.

Stuart's heart started to pound. He had not felt this nervous since he'd asked Randy Ross to go steady in the sixth

160

grade. This was a perfect opportunity and yet he could not go through with it. There was no way he could walk in, sit down and introduce himself. Certainly not with Mr. Cowboy sitting a few feet away. The whole idea was too embarrassing, or at least contained too much potential for embarrassment.

Feeling short of breath and wondering if all this pounding was bad for his heart, he continued slowly down the block. He was unable to introduce himself, but equally reluctant to depart when she was so close. What the hell was wrong with him anyway? He was an adult now, not a teenager. If you wanted to talk to someone, you went up and introduced yourself, right?

Right. He stopped and turned around. It had started to rain harder now. He could feel the drops soak into his shirt and dampen his shoulders. He would go back and introduce himself, plain and simple.

Or maybe he would go in and just pretend he needed to get out of the rain. Maybe *she'd* recognize *him*.

He was about twenty feet from the laundromat when she suddenly came out and started walking quickly toward him on the sidewalk.

His heart began to pound again. Just say hello, he told himself. Here she comes. Now, Stuart, now!

She came, she passed, she went. He'd said nothing; wasn't sure she'd even noticed him. She was holding the umbrella and looking down at the sidewalk. He turned and watched her go down the block and into the Love Store.

Perfect! He could go in and buy a box of Pampers. That was almost the same as having Claire with him. They could start chatting while they waited in line at the cashier.

He was almost in the door when he realized he didn't have his wallet. Damn it! And now it was really starting to pour. He stood outside and looked in the doorway at the aisles of shampoo and makeup, but couldn't see her.

Boom! A sudden crack of thunder made him jump. Jesus,

on top of how his heart was already beating he'd probably have a coronary. Rainwater had matted down his hair and was running into his eyes. His shirt clung to his shoulders and he could feel water seeping down his back and into his underwear. This was ridiculous. Why was he standing in the rain following a woman he didn't even know?

He took a step back and noticed that people passing on the sidewalk were giving him strange looks. They think I'm just another crazy, he thought. I'm not crazy, he wanted to tell them.

Just slightly confused.

22

BACK in the apartment he changed out of his wet clothes and dried his hair with a towel. He was bothered by what had just happened. It wasn't so disturbing that he had followed her to the laundromat, but what really concerned him was how, standing in the rain outside the pharmacy, he'd been unable to leave. He felt like he'd been possessed by a demon spirit. Soaked to the skin, he'd finally left, but he wondered what would have happened had he stayed.

He was about to get to work when 0801 lit up. He answered it.

"Stuart, this is Sam. Claire had an accident. You better come over."

His heart hopped, skipped and jumped. "Is she okay?"

"We think so," Sam said. "She had a pretty bad scare and she's got a cut that's going to need attention."

"What happened?"

"She fell against a radiator."

"I'll be right there."

Stuart grabbed a rain slicker and ran. By the time he

reached IFIL he was out of breath and gasping for air. He pushed impatiently on the intercom until he was let in. Sam was sitting on a couch near the entrance, cradling Claire in his arms and holding a gauze pad against her nose. A teaching assistant named Deena was also there, trying to comfort her. As soon as Claire saw Stuart she began to whimper and stretched her arms out toward him.

"Daddy, Daddy."

Stuart squatted down and kissed her. The gauze pad had turned blood-red in the center.

"What happened?" he asked Sam.

"She ran into the radiator. No one saw it happen. But look." Sam lifted the gauze pad. Claire's nose was bloody from a cut that went straight up her nostril. Stuart tried to touch it and she screamed. The nostril was severed clear through.

"Holy shit," Stuart said.

"Fall down," Claire whimpered. "Scared."

Stuart took her from Sam and hugged her. "It's okay, hon, everything's okay." He turned to the teacher. "Have you got a phone?"

"Sure." Sam took him into the office. Holding Claire in one arm, Stuart dialed Laurie's number.

"Lauren Fine's office," Bridget, her secretary, answered.

"Bridget, it's Stuart. Is she around?"

"She's in a meeting with Peter."

"Better get her. This is important."

A few seconds later Laurie got on the phone. "What is it?"

"Claire fell down and cut her nose. She seems okay, but I'm sure she's going to need stitches. What's the doctor's name again?"

"Benson. He's on Eighty-sixth. I'll have Bridget look up the address for you. How bad is the cut?"

"Her nostril is severed."

He heard the sharp intake of Laurie's breath. "I don't want her to go to Benson. She has to see a plastic surgeon."

"Why?"

"It's her face, Stuart. Do you want her to be scarred for life?"

"Okay, who?"

"Hold on and I'll call Dr. Omura, the one who took that mole off my lip."

Stuart held the phone and the gauze against Claire's nose. It was the first time he had seen his daughter's blood. It felt worse than if he himself had been bleeding.

Laurie got back on. "Okay, Omura can see her. Sixty-six Central Park West. I'll meet you there."

As Stuart hung up, Sam slid a form onto the desk in front of him. "Could you sign this?"

"What is it?" Stuart asked.

"Better read it."

Still holding Claire in his arms, Stuart read the form. It was a release clearing IFIL of any responsibility for Claire's injuries.

Stuart looked up at Sam. "I can't sign this."

"We're really not supposed to let Claire go until you do," Sam said.

"Are you serious?"

"That's our policy."

Stuart was half-incredulous and half-incensed. "Look, my kid is bleeding. I'm taking her to the doctor. If she's hurt then as far as I'm concerned you are responsible." Stuart carried Claire past the teacher. Sam made no attempt to stop him, which was lucky since Stuart was prepared to duke it out for his daughter's legal rights. Near the door he picked up her stroller and then carried everything out to the street and hailed a cab.

Laurie was in the waiting room of Dr. Omura's office when they arrived. Claire immediately reached for her and began to whimper again. The doctor, a short smiling Asian man wearing a white medical jacket, interrupted another appointment to briefly inspect Claire's nose. Claire screamed when he touched it and the doctor backed away.

"Did she lose consciousness or vomit?" he asked.

"They didn't say anything about that," Stuart said.

"It will take only two stitches," the doctor said. "Let me finish with this other appointment and we will do it."

He returned to his office. Stuart and Laurie sat down in the waiting room. Claire sat on Laurie's lap with her eyes squeezed shut. The bleeding had stopped enough so that they only had to dab under her nose occasionally. Laurie rocked her gently.

"What radiator did she hit?" she asked.

"The one in the classroom," Stuart said. "No one saw it happen. They wanted me to sign a release form stating that I wouldn't hold the center responsible."

"Did you?"

"Of course not."

Laurie shook her head. "God, I can't believe that."

Meanwhile, Claire opened her eyes and started to slide down from Laurie's lap. "Books," she said, pointing at some magazines. A few seconds later she was sitting on the floor, looking at them.

Stuart looked at Laurie. "I guess she's okay."

"Just wait," Laurie said. "I have a feeling the fun hasn't begun."

In the waiting room, Doctor Omura gave Claire a shot of Demerol. "It will make her groggy and lessen the discomfort," he said. "Also, she'll be less likely to remember anything tomorrow."

Omura went back into his office and saw another patient. Stuart and Laurie waited more than an hour while Claire tried to fight the drowsiness caused by the drug. Finally when she could no longer keep her eyes open, Dr. Omura said they would begin.

What followed was the most horrifying experience Stuart had had in years. As soon as they brought Claire into the

166

doctor's office, she was wide awake again, as if the Demerol had no effect at all. She screamed in terror and clawed at Laurie as Dr. Omura and his nurse swaddled her in a sheet and laid her on the examination table.

Omura turned to Stuart. "You will hold her head. She must not move or she will hurt herself."

The next thing Stuart knew, he was standing at the end of the examination table, cradling Claire's head in his arms like a football. Laurie was at the other end of the table trying to hold Claire's legs down. Claire was screaming and twisting like a small wild animal. Stuart was amazed at the strength in her little body.

"You must do better," Dr. Omura told them.

Stuart held her tighter and the doctor painted Claire's nose with brown iodine solution. The nurse then handed him a hypodermic. Omura tested it, then glanced at Stuart. He's telling me this is going to be rough, Stuart thought. He held Claire's head tighter and looked away.

A moment later Claire screamed louder than ever and fought savagely. It took all of Stuart's strength to hold her head still. He had to squeeze so hard he was afraid he was hurting her. It made him feel sick. Then he looked and saw that blood had splattered everywhere. He felt even sicker.

He did not watch Omura put the stitches in. He'd already seen enough. He gripped Claire's head and held it still. She continued to fight and scream. Stuart closed his eyes and concentrated on breathing regularly, mindful that he didn't want to faint.

In the cab home, they were silent. The experience had exhausted them. Claire sat on Laurie's lap, sucking her thumb. Her nose was swollen black and yellow from the anaesthetic. Dried blood clung to her nostrils.

At home they put her on the living room couch and let her watch *Sesame Street* tapes until she fell asleep. Neither Stuart nor Laurie had much of an appetite. Around ten

Stuart made some scrambled eggs. Around eleven they went to bed.

He was just starting to doze off when Laurie said, "I don't want her to go back there tomorrow."

Stuart opened his eyes. "She has to. We don't have any choice."

"I'll stay home."

"And what will you do the day after tomorrow?"

"I'll resign. I hate this."

"Hate what?"

"Feeling so helpless, so out of control when it comes to Claire. I knew something like this would happen if we left her with strangers."

Stuart rolled over and put his arms around her. "Listen, what happened today could have just as easily happened while you or I were watching her. She's fallen down and hurt herself before. I once stepped on her hand when I didn't see her on the floor behind me. These things happen."

Laurie burrowed into his arms. She sniffed and trembled. "She could have really been hurt."

"I know. We were lucky. A lot of it's luck. You can't control everything."

"But you have to try. You have to control as much as you can."

"You can't. You'll turn into Mrs. Messing, calling parents and threatening them if they send their kids back to school too soon."

"I understand it now."

Stuart hugged her. "Listen, if you would feel better staying home with Claire, you should."

Laurie rolled onto her back and blew her nose. "Could we afford it?"

"I'll go back to a firm."

"How could I just quit?" she asked. "I worked my ass off for eight years to get where I am now. I'm vested. I've got profit sharing. How could I throw it away?"

168

"You wouldn't have to. Maybe you'll only take off until Claire's in school full-time."

Laurie looked at him in the dark. "Suppose I kept working and *you* took off the time to watch her."

"I don't think we could live on your salary alone," Stuart said.

"But just pretend, Stuart," she said. "Pretend I did earn enough. Would you be willing to give up work for three years to take care of her?"

Stuart had to admit the answer was, "No."

"See? It's not fair," Laurie said.

"But it doesn't bother me as much as it bothers you."

"It's still not fair."

Stuart thought of Claire squirming and thrashing on the examination table, terrified, too young to comprehend that the pain the doctor was inflicting was for her own good. He reached for Laurie but she didn't want to come to him. "Listen," he said, "You're right. It's not fair."

23

B Y working at home he could help ease the burden of caring for Claire, but there was nothing Stuart could do about the burden of Laurie's work or the pressure she put on herself. All of which had a direct affect on their love life. Since Claire's birth it seemed as if sex with Laurie had the half-life of a rapidly deteriorating radioactive isotope. They talked briefly about seeing a therapist, but that meant getting a baby-sitter one evening a week and spending even more time away from Claire. Besides, neither of them wanted to admit the problem was that large.

So they planned a vacation instead. Their first real vacation since Claire was born.

"Just wait until we get to the beach," Laurie said. "We'll build fires at night and cuddle. I won't be so exhausted from work. We'll have lots of good sex."

"What about Claire?"

"We'll put her to bed early."

They rented a sun-bleached wood contemporary with skylights and a cathedral ceiling in the woods north of East

Hampton. The house had a deck with a Weber grill and brand-new outdoor furniture. The kitchen had a dishwasher and a refrigerator with an icemaker. The living room had a fireplace. One bedroom and a bath downstairs. Two bedrooms and a bath upstairs. Stuart and Laurie moved into one of the upstairs bedrooms and put Claire in the other. They put her to bed and opened the windows to let in the cool night air. She looked tiny in the big bed.

"Noises," she said.

"It's only the crickets," Stuart said, kissing her nose. It had healed with amazing speed, leaving just a trace of a scar, which Omura said would probably disappear by the time she was eight.

A second later a dog barked.

"Monster," Claire said.

"No, hon, it was just a dog."

"Scared," Claire said, her lower lip quivering.

Laurie kissed her. "Don't be a silly. Nothing's going to hurt you here."

They left her door open, and went down the hall to their bedroom and undressed.

"I like the feel of this house," Stuart said, getting into the queen-sized platform bed. "It's functional, not pretentious."

Next to him, Laurie lay quietly on her back.

"You want to play tennis in the morning or can't you wait to get to the beach?" Stuart asked.

Laurie didn't answer.

"What is it?" Stuart asked.

"Listen," she whispered. "What's that noise?"

Stuart listened. He heard faint squeakings and poppings. "If I had to guess, I'd say it's just the house," he whispered back. "It heats up during the day and cools down at night. When things heat up they expand, when they cool they contract."

"Houses expand and contract?"

"I'm theorizing that the materials they're made of do," Stuart said. He got the feeling Laurie didn't accept this as a suitable answer. She became quiet again. Stuart leaned toward her and kissed her ear, sliding one hand over her breast.

"What's that?" Laurie asked.

Stuart paused and listened. He heard scratching sounds.

"It's probably a raccoon or something," he said. "Just some animal. Relax, Woofee. We're way out in the woods. No one's going to bother us."

He tried to get romantic, but she was too tense.

"Laurie, nothing's going to happen out here," he said. "It's not New York. The woods aren't filled with muggers." He kissed her on the lips, but she did not open her mouth.

"I'm sorry," she said. "I'm just not used to all these noises."

"But there's nothing out there," Stuart said. No sooner had the words left his mouth than they heard a rapid series of knocks. Stuart stiffened.

"What was that?" Laurie gasped.

"I don't know," Stuart said.

"It sounded like knocking."

Stuart took a deep breath. "I'll go see."

He got out of bed and pulled on some pants. Who knocked in the middle of the night in the middle of the woods? Burglars trying to see if anyone was home before they ransacked the place, that's who. Stuart swallowed. He realized he hadn't put on a shirt or shoes. How could he defend his family barefoot and with no shirt on? Then again, what did he think he could do even if he was wearing them?

He went downstairs slowly. Don't scare yourself, he thought, it's probably just a neighbor. But downstairs, there was no one at the front door and no one at the door to the deck either. Stuart considered going outside to look, then changed his mind and went through the downstairs rooms, making sure the doors were locked and windows closed. He went back upstairs.

"What was it?" Laurie asked.

"I don't know," he said, taking his pants off. "There was no one there."

"Great. We've rented a haunted house," Laurie said.

"Stop it, Laurie. Whatever it was, it was harmless. Now I thought the idea was to come out here, relax and make love."

"Sure," Laurie said. "And I'm really in the mood."

If the frequency of their lovemaking didn't increase, their entertaining did. They couldn't help it. They owed too many invitations. Since Claire's birth they'd hardly had anyone over for dinner. Not only that, but the vacation house had that terrific deck and outdoor furniture. How could they not take advantage of it?

Guests came for the day, for the weekend, for three days, whatever. A steady stream of friends who needed drinks and shish kebab, beer and burgers, clean sheets and towels, golf, tennis and fishing partners. They tracked sand through the house and left dirty towels on the bathroom floor and dirty glasses in the sink.

Stuart and Laurie cooked, cleaned, ran the washer and dryer, shopped and did errands in town every day. Each night their sleep was disturbed by the "ghost" who knocked, until Stuart discovered that it was the ice maker in the refrigerator popping new cubes. He disconnected it and started buying ice by the bag, but somehow it still didn't help his and Laurie's sex life. One morning while preparing the guest bedroom for the next couple, he found a crumpled-up tube of Koromex spermicidal jelly on the floor near the bed. At least someone was having fun.

Dave and Joan came for the day and brought their kids, Brent, four, and Stephen, seven. They all went to the beach, put up their umbrellas, spread their beach towels and applied Bain De Soleil. The boys played with Claire while the women lay in the sun and the men sat in beach chairs with unopened books in their laps.

173

"She likes older men," Dave said, as the boys showed Claire how to make a sand castle.

Stuart nodded, but he wasn't really paying attention. Instead he was staring covertly through his sunglasses at a darkly tanned young woman lying on her stomach about twenty-five feet away. Her string top was undone, revealing an absence of unsightly tan lines. In the midday heat, sweat collected in Stuart's belly button and his nose was full of the aroma of suntan lotion. He imagined himself a wraith with undeniable sexual appeal, floating almost weightless beside her, sliding her bikini bottoms down over her lotioned legs, hearing the sharp intake of her breath followed by pleasured purring as he enveloped her in a misty cloud of arousal, gliding softly into her under the hot sun, warm sweat and suntan lotion lubricating their bodies until they climaxed intensely. Then he would float away, leaving her wondering if it had been a dream.

"You don't happen to know where the market opened this morning, do you?" Dave asked.

Stuart shook his head and carefully lowered his book to his lap. It was a good thing he wasn't wearing a tight bathing suit. Screw the stock market. He could feel the hormones brewing inside him, fermenting in the heat of the sun. That's what lying on the beach does, he thought. It turns you into a teenager again.

"Want to go for a walk?" Dave asked.

"Sure." He and Dave headed east. It was late afternoon of a midweek day and the beach was not crowded. Groups of women with children dotted the shore, usually in front of a wooden beach house. As they walked, Stuart told Dave how he and Eliot had discovered Carol's affair.

"I just can't understand why she'd do it," Stuart said.

"Sometimes it just happens," Dave said.

"I don't know," Stuart said. "I have trouble with the concept of it just happening. You don't *just* have an affair.

Maybe you become attracted to someone. But you don't just accidentally sleep with them. You decide to. It is a conscious decision."

Dave picked up a red and white crab's claw and inspected it as they walked. "But sometimes it's a conscious decision that just happens. Not everyone is as self-aware as you. I mean it. Some people don't think these things out."

"I don't believe that," Stuart said, although it did make him recall his recent, peculiar experiences at the Pink Poodle and in the pouring rain outside the pharmacy on Broadway while *she* shopped inside.

"Listen," Dave said. "Suppose I told you you're wrong. Suppose I told you it's even happened to me."

Stuart was quiet for a moment. He'd known Dave since college and it was in college that Dave and Joan had started going together.

"When?" he asked finally.

"Swear to God you'll never tell anyone? Not even Laurie?"

"You already know the answer."

"Sondra."

Stuart stared for a second at him. Sondra had been Bingham's assistant comptroller. Young, with curly brown hair and big brown eyes. The three of them had occasionally lunched together until Sondra was hired away by Deloitte Haskins & Sells.

"She's married," Stuart said.

"Not anymore."

"But she was then and so were, and are, you."

"I swear to God, Stuart, if you ever breath a word of this."

"Save it."

"You never noticed anything between us?" Dave asked. Stuart shook his head.

Dave seemed pleased. "We were careful. You don't know what it's like. You're attracted to someone. You see them every day. You work with them every day. You go on business trips together. It just builds and builds."

"How long did it last?"

"Only a few times."

"How come?"

"Because that's all it meant to us. It didn't signify the beginning of a relationship. It was just something overdue at the end. She was leaving the company and we knew it wouldn't lead to complications."

"And that's why I was always asked along at lunch," Stuart said.

Dave smiled. "We enjoyed your company, but it was also a good cover."

"And at night you'd go home and sleep with Joan?"

"Something like that."

"I can't believe I never noticed," Stuart said.

"If you're not looking, it's harder to see."

They walked along the beach without talking for a while.

"Eleven o'clock," Dave whispered. Stuart looked ahead and slightly to his left. A darkly tanned woman was reclining in a beach chair, her head tilted back and her eyes closed, luxuriating in the afternoon sun. Topless. Her breasts glistening with suntan oil, the skin nearly as brown as the rest of her body. A man lay stomach down on a blanket next to her, reading.

Dave and Stuart passed within fifteen yards, their eyes riveted on the scene, neither of them daring to speak. The woman, she was blond of course, never opened her eyes. The man never looked up from his book.

"Jesus," Dave groaned when they were past.

"Nice," Stuart said.

"You see how brown they were?" Dave said. "Bet they've spent the whole summer on the beach while we bust our humps to make a few bucks."

"A few?"

"Relative to what they probably have," Dave said. "And they have it without having to work. You know how many

176

vacations I've had to cancel because of work in the last three years? We were going to take three weeks and go to Australia. Then it got cut back to seventeen days so we figured Japan. Then it got cut to ten days so we picked Hawaii. Then it turned out I had a meeting in LA so we figured we'd go to San Francisco for five days. We wound up taking three days at Vail. I swear, I probably cancel two vacations for every one that I take. What I wouldn't give to spend a whole summer on a beach."

They walked down past the jetties and came to some mansions set back in the dunes. The beach here was empty except for one couple. A muscular man lay on his side on the sand, his head propped on his elbow, gazing silently at the waves. A young woman lay with her head on his waist, topless.

David and Stuart passed silently. The woman's eyes followed them.

"Bet he's some semifamous jock and she's a rich sports groupie," Dave said when they were out of earshot. "God, when you think about it . . ." He didn't finish the sentence.

"It never stops," Stuart said.

"Not for as long as ye both shall live."

"What do you think it is that makes the thought of sleeping with another woman so different from sleeping with your own wife?" Stuart asked.

"Ego."

"That's all?"

"I think that's all *we* are," Dave said. "It's the same thing that makes us stay up all night going after deals when the rest of the world has gone to bed. It's what drives us. I once read a study that said the happiest marriages were those where the men were not great achievers. They were" —Dave paused to work up the disdain in his voice— "content."

They stopped and stood side by side at the water's edge, looking out at the horizon and letting the waves wash over their feet.

"You want to know the truth?" Dave asked. "If you tell me that you've been faithful I'll honestly be surprised. With all the traveling you did."

"You never meet anyone on the road," Stuart said.

"No, you usually bring them with you from New York."

"I imagine that could get kind of expensive."

"No way," Dave said. "You use your frequent-flyer miles. The company pays for your ticket. Frequent flyer pays for hers. The hotel and meals are expensed. What does it cost you?"

Way out on the horizon, a trawler was heading back toward Montauk. Did the airlines know they were boosting infidelity? He wondered what impressed Dave more, the illicit sex, or the fact that it was all paid for?

"My father used to say that eighty percent of all men cheat in America," Dave said. "The other twenty percent cheat overseas."

They started walking back along the water's edge. The orange sun glared in their eyes, their shadows stretched behind them.

"Suppose you wanted to try to remain faithful," Stuart said.

Dave shrugged. "I don't know. Maybe you pretend your wife is a different woman. Ask her if she'll dress up differently or act differently. Play fantasy games. Go on sexual adventures. Join the Mile High Club."

"The what?"

"You don't know what the Mile High Club is?"

"Don't give me that," Stuart said. "Whatever it is I bet you just found out about it last week."

"You do it in an airplane."

Stuart looked at him.

"Well, it's different," Dave said.

"In the seats?"

"The bathroom."

"Ridiculous."

"Maybe, but it's kind of a kick to think about. I mean,

what else do we have to look forward to? Another hundred thousand in salary? More unfriendly takeovers? Retirement? Imagine telling my son someday that he was conceived in the bathroom of a jet?"

"What if you have a daughter?"

"I guess I wouldn't tell her."

"So that's what you look forward to?"

Dave looked down at him. "Don't be condescending, my friend. We're all in this together."

They returned to their encampment by the sea. Laurie was sitting with Joan amid the blankets and coolers. Claire was taking a nap under the umbrella. Stephen and Brent were making another sand castle. Dave sat down on the blanket next to Joan and kissed her on the cheek. Family man, Stuart thought. Family *men*.

24

———

H E returned from vacation more intent than ever on meeting *her*. She was separate now in his mind from his relationship with Laurie. Laurie was his wife, the mother of his daughter. He would never leave either of them. He would never be unfaithful in the sense that he would ever care about another woman as much as he cared for Laurie. But if Laurie could harmlessly flirt, if Dave could sleep with Sondra simply because it was destined with no strings attached, then he could at least meet *her*. This was not an emotional situation, it was psychobiological. As with David and Sondra, it was something he had to get out of his system.

He just hoped *she* had to get it out of her system too.

Dusty pink marble columns stood in the lobby of the Excelsior Arms. Seventy years of scuff marks dulled the black tile floors and the dust on the chandelier was so heavy it seemed as if the glass had grown fur. The place even smelled old. A frail old lady with thick glasses sat on a worn-out couch and watched him. The glasses made her eyes look unnaturally large, as if she had a permanently horrified look on her face. Stuart took a deep breath. If I lived here, I might feel that way too, he thought.

The hotel desk was enclosed in thick, bulletproof plastic, the sort of decoration one usually found in inner-city liquor stores. Inside, a young Indian man sat watching a game show on a small black and white television set.

"I'd like to look at a room." Stuart spoke though a dozen small holes drilled in the plastic.

"For how long?" the Indian man asked. He was wearing a blue checked short-sleeve shirt.

"A couple of weeks. If I take it."

"With a toilet?"

This intrigued him. "What if I say no?"

"You share one down the hall."

"I'll spring for a toilet."

"Spring, sir?"

"I'll take one with a toilet."

The man nodded and perused the wallful of mail slots before selecting a key. "That will be two hundred and seventy-six dollars please."

"I'd like to see the room first," Stuart said.

The Indian man scowled. "All right. Wait a minute." He left the desk and went into an office. A moment later he returned with an elderly gray-haired Indian woman wearing a blue sari. She stayed at the desk while the Indian man let himself out of the plastic cage and led Stuart to the elevator.

Stuart was appalled by the decrepitness of the hotel. A damp, dank smell hung in the halls. Greenish institutional paint peeled off the walls and in some places the carpeting was worn clear to the wooden floor beneath. As the man led him down the hallway, Stuart watched the door numbers carefully. But they were headed toward the back of the hotel and from there he had no idea how the rooms in the front were numbered.

The room the man showed him was painted dull yellow.

181

It had a scarred wooden bed, a chest of drawers, one spindly wooden chair and a floor lamp.

"Have you got anything on a higher floor?" Stuart asked. "Something that gets some sunlight?"

The Indian man scowled again. He probably wasn't used to people being so choosy about their rooms. "I think there's one on eight."

They returned to the desk, got another key and took the elevator up. The room on the eighth floor was in the front of the building. The sun streamed in through the broken venetian blinds, and across the street Stuart could see the French doors of his own apartment. They were in room 819. If the room numbers were uniform floor by floor, then *hers* would be 921.

"You'll take this one?" the Indian man asked.

Stuart shook his head. "I was hoping for something a little nicer. There's another hotel on Seventy-sixth Street I want to check."

"That's a bad hotel, sir. Full of drug addicts and prostitution."

"If that's the case, I'll be back."

He went home and waited by the French doors until he saw *her* shade rise. Today she did not open the window and lean out, but she was naked as usual. He reached for the phone. His heart was beating madly and his throat felt tight as he dialed the number of the Excelsior Arms. Twice he misdialed and had to try again. Finally he got it right and the Indian man answered.

"Room nine twenty-one please."

"Hold on."

He heard a series of clicks and then a woman answered. "Hello?" She had a deep, languid voice and an accent that he couldn't place.

"Hello," he said.

"Murray?" she said.

"No, this is someone you don't know."

182

"Who?"

"Well, first let me ask you something. Are you the woman with the tall blond lady friend who has a crew cut?"

"Why, yes. Who is this?"

"My name is Stuart and I live across the street." And I'm just about to have a heart attack, he thought, feeling the pounding in his chest.

She responded slowly. "Oh, I see. Which one are you?"

"What?"

"Which building, darling? There are two or three faces that I always see."

"Oh, uh, I live at four ninety-six, on the seventh floor."

"Uh-huh." She was completely blasé.

"Listen, I hope you're not freaked out by this," he said, although she did not sound at all freaked out. If anyone was, it was he.

"Oh, no, this year has been too freaky already. You couldn't freak me out anymore."

"Oh, good."

"The white-brick building?" she asked.

"What?"

"Is that the one you live in?"

"No, no. I'm in the red-brick building next to it."

"With those lovely French doors and that little balcony?"

"You could call it that, but I wouldn't put more than a flower box on it."

"I've seen you watching me," she said.

I cannot believe I am doing this, he thought.

"I guess you wonder why I'm always at home," he said.

"Oh, are you a producer of something?" she asked.

It sounded like a non sequitur. He could only imagine that she knew a producer who worked at home. "Are you in the theater?" he asked back.

"Actually I design clothes and do free-lance modeling. But I'm really tired of that. I want to get back into something normal and nine-to-five."

"I noticed you seem to keep strange hours."

"You did?" She sounded more surprised than he expected.

"Sometimes you get up at four in the afternoon."

"How do you know that?"

He could tell she was not pleased to hear this. Could he have been wrong all these months? Was it possible that she didn't think he could see her naked? But she said she'd seen him watching her.

"Well, the shade goes up and then the window fogs like someone is taking a shower."

"What else have you seen?"

"Well, I have to admit I've seen you in the nude."

"Oh."

"Hey, listen . . ." Why had he told her *that*?

He expected her to hang up or become angry, but she only sighed. "I should have guessed. Do you know that there is a man in the white building who stands by his window and plays with himself? And there's one who uses binoculars."

"No, I didn't."

"I guess I should really be more discreet."

"Well, I don't know."

"Do you like watching me?"

He could imagine her at that moment, pacing back and forth across the room, the phone nestled in the crook of her neck. Naked. He was talking to a naked woman. "You're a very attractive woman."

"Thank you."

"This may sound strange," Stuart said. "But I'd like to know more about your life. I mean, sometimes I see you get out of a cab at seven in the morning."

"You must watch a lot."

"I can work and look out the window at the same time."

"And you work at seven in the morning?"

"When I have to make calls overseas."

"I do go out all night sometimes, but I'm really tired of that life. I mean, it really goes nowhere and just wears you out. You don't meet anyone. You don't develop any lasting relationships. Nothing you can profit from. And so many people are getting that awful disease. It's so frightening. I really need to make some money now. I'm trying to find a nine-to-five job."

"In what?"

"Oh, sales, anything really, just to make some money."

"I wish I knew someone who could help you."

"What sort of business are you in?"

"I, uh, manage money."

"Oh? How?"

"People give me money and I invest it for them. As long as they get good returns, they're happy."

"Is this something you had to go to school to learn?"

"I sort of learned it on the side, actually. I used to be an options trader, but I wanted to work for myself so I gradually got into this."

"And you can do it right out of your home? You don't need an office?"

"Well, this is an office. If you saw it, you'd understand."

"Most people would love to work out of their homes."

"I don't know. I thought I would, but now I'm not so sure. I miss interacting with people. It's funny; I originally started working out of the house because I found my time was being taken up by too many stupid things. But now I sort of miss some of them."

"What do you miss?"

"Going to lunch. I know that probably sounds trite, but all my old lunch buddies are down on Wall Street and it's just too far to go. Uh, actually, that's one of the reasons I called. As I said before, this will sound crazy, but maybe you'd like to have lunch with me sometime."

"Okay."

He was surprised that she'd agreed. "How does tomorrow sound?"

"Okay, I guess. Why don't you give me a call around eleven?"

"You sure that's not too early? I don't want to wake you."

"Oh, don't worry. I never really sleep. I take a lot of naps. Sometimes I spend all day in bed. I know I shouldn't. I'm trying not to. I really have to make some money."

"You know, I never asked your name."

"Oh, uh, Charmine."

"Char, mine. That's pretty."

"And your name was Fred?"

"Stuart."

"Okay, Stuart, call me tomorrow."

"I will."

He hung up the phone and sat at his desk, staring at the Quotron. Had he done it? Had he actually made a date with *her*? He couldn't believe it.

25

THAT night, just before going to bed, he went into his office and looked across the street. It occurred to him that *she* might have one of those teenage boys over. He didn't know why that should bother him, but it did. He stood by the French doors and watched. The light was on in her room and the shade was drawn. Her silhouette passed in front of it a few times. She seemed to be alone.

He went back to the bedroom. Laurie was sitting up with some pillows behind her back, reading *Vogue*. He got into bed and pulled the blanket over his shoulder as if he was trying to hide from her.

"Con Ed is coming tomorrow between eleven and two," she said.

He sat up. "What? Why?"

"You know that gas leak in the oven? I smelled it again this morning. I called them from work and they said they'd send someone to look at it."

"That's ridiculous. I've never smelled gas in the kitchen. They're going to come up here for nothing."

"I always smell it."

"Shouldn't you have asked me first?" Stuart asked. "What if I'm busy tomorrow between eleven and two?"

"Are you?"

"Well, no."

Laurie smiled. "Then there's no problem."

He couldn't concentrate on work the next morning. He stood by the French doors, waiting to see a sign of wakefulness in Charmine's room or for the arrival of a Con Edison truck on the street below. Why was he having lunch with her? What was his ultimate goal? To become her friend? Lover? Wasn't he kidding himself? Every time he let his mind wander, it led him into a sun-washed room. And she was always there, and always naked. Why couldn't he just admit that he wanted to sleep with her?

Because maybe he didn't.

Oh, bullshit.

The phone rang. He picked it up.

"I'm not going to make it," Eliot said. He sounded long-distance. "I can't stand it. I just want it to end."

"Where are you?" Stuart asked.

"On some asshole's private yacht in San Diego Bay. I feel like throwing myself over the side. The torment is killing me."

"Eliot, please don't talk this way."

"I'm serious."

"I know you're serious, but you have a long life ahead of you. You're a great guy. You'll meet plenty of terrific women."

"I won't. My shoulders are too narrow."

"What?"

"I don't have broad shoulders. You look at Carol's body. It's perfect. It's more than perfect. It's perfect plus three extra inches in all the right places. You know what the male equivalent of her body would be?"

"Let me guess. Arnold Schwarzenegger."

"Exactly. And look what she wound up with. A five-foot-nine-inch schlump with narrow shoulders and negative muscle tone. We've been mismatched since day one."

"Carol is not that shallow."

"Don't you see? It has nothing to do with shallowness. It has to do with basic biological compatability."

"Eliot, you're crazy. But just suppose you're right. What does it matter now?"

"It matters because this is my life, you idiot!" Eliot shouted from San Diego Bay. "You think I could ever be happy with the female equivalent of me? After knowing a woman like Carol? I'm doomed. This is the end. It's all downhill from here. I wish I could go to sleep and never wake up."

"Wait a minute," Stuart said. "If you really believe that, look at Bruce Springsteen. He built himself up physically and married a model."

Eliot laughed. "That's a great comparison. Me and Bruce Springsteen. Springsteen is a national hero. A multi-millionaire and a rock star. It's like comparing Spam to filet mignon. Besides, I hate to exercise."

Stuart only half heard him. He was watching Charmine's window and thought he saw something.

"Stu? You there?"

"Yes." It was just the reflection of the sun.

"What am I gonna do?"

"You're gonna keep going. Finish the trip. Come home. Take it day by day. You'll make it."

"I don't know, man. I really can't describe what this is like. It's constant torment. I just want to be unconscious. I go to bed at night and wish I didn't have to wake up in the morning."

"You can make it, Eliot. You're a smart, good-looking, successful guy. There are a million women in this city who dream of a guy like you. As soon as you're ready, you'll have your pick. I promise you."

"You really think so?"

189

"Yes, absolutely."

"You're a good man, Stu," Eliot said. "Do you mind if I call again and curse at you? This really helps."

"Call as much as you want. It's fine with me."

"You're a friend, Stu. A real friend."

Eleven A.M. arrived, then noon. Eliot didn't call back and there was no sign of life in Charmine's room. Stuart didn't know what to do. Suppose he took Charmine out to lunch and Eliot called again and was in bad shape? Suppose Con Ed came and he wasn't there? They might call Laurie at her office. Then he'd have to explain where he'd been.

At 12:15 the doorbell rang.

"Who is it?"

"Con Ed."

He pulled open the door and let in a young man wearing a baseball cap, T-shirt and jeans. Around his waist was a heavy belt weighed down with a flashlight, pliers and other tools.

"Someone called and said there was a gas leak?"

"Well, it was my wife actually," Stuart said. "I've never smelled gas myself." He wanted to make certain that he did not receive any of the blame for this unnecessary visit.

The man from Con Ed walked toward the kitchen. Con Ed men and exterminators never had to be told where the kitchen was. They must have had a sixth sense about these things. "She pregnant?"

"Sorry?"

"Your wife, is she pregnant?"

"Not that I know of," Stuart said, following him.

"Ninety percent of the time pregnant women are right," the man from Con Ed said. In the kitchen he reached around the sides of the stove and pulled the top off, revealing the burners plus small mounds of unidentifiable black substances and strands of fossilized spaghetti. Stuart felt a twinge of embarrassment, but the man from Con Ed didn't blink.

"She was pregnant a couple of years ago," Stuart said. "And she's been talking about this leak for a long time."

The man from Con Ed nodded. He reached to his belt and unhooked a plant mister filled with soapy water, then sprayed it on the metal hose that led from the gas outlet to the stove.

"They can smell stuff," he said. "Guess it has to do with some inborn type of thing to protect the young one. Know what I mean?"

Stuart nodded, although he wasn't sure.

"Here you go," the man from Con Ed said, pointing at a large soapy bubble growing out of the place where the metal tube connected with the stove's burner. "I'm telling ya, better check and see if she's pregnant."

The man from Con Ed turned off the gas and fixed the leak. Then he left. Stuart realized he didn't even have to pay him. He dialed Laurie's number at work.

"Hello?"

"The man from Con Ed came. Are you pregnant?"

"Would you repeat that please?" Laurie said.

"The man from Con Ed said pregnant women can detect minute gas leaks that no one else can smell. It turns out we had just such a leak. Hence, you must be pregnant."

"I don't think I am," Laurie said.

"You mean you're not sure?"

"When did I have my last period?"

"You don't remember?"

"All I know is that it was a long time ago. Before we went on vacation."

"But after you got back from Portugal."

"I wish I could remember."

"You're not serious," Stuart said.

"Peter wants all the sales figures for the last eight months correlated to our advertising buys per region. Martha says she can't go to Du Pont, so I have to find someone else or go myself. One of my people just resigned this morning and another says she has to change her vacation plans because her sister just had premature twins. I have a new product presentation tomorrow morning and I have to go over to BBDO this afternoon to see a rough cut of a new ad. And you think that on top of all that I can remember the last time I menstruated?"

"Maybe you ought to get tested."

"Remind me tonight and I'll try to remember. If I can't I'll have a test. In the meantime, don't forget to pick up Claire. I've got a million things to do. I probably won't be home until around eight. Bye."

He hung up and looked across the street. His heart began to pound again. There was nothing between them now. He reached for the phone and dialed the number of the hotel. When the Indian man answered, he asked for room 921.

He heard the normal clicks and noises. Then the Indian man got back on again. "She's not there."

But she must be! he thought.

"Are you sure?"

"She hasn't come back yet," he said.

"You mean, she went out this morning?"

The man sighed. "From last night, sir."

"Oh."

"Would you care to leave a message, sir?"

"Uh, no. That's all right. Thanks." He hung up and walked over to his computer and flicked it on with an impatient snap of his wrist. Damn it!

26

THE next morning at 9:30 he called the hotel again and asked for Charmine's room. The Indian man said she was not in.

"Are you sure?" Stuart asked.

"Yes, I'm sure."

"You saw her go out this morning?"

"I saw her go out last night, sir."

"She said she'd be in. Is it possible that she might have come in and you didn't see her?"

The Indian man sighed. "Just a minute, sir."

Stuart listened to the familiar sound of clicks and pops. The Excelsior Arms' phone system must have predated the Civil War. The man came back on. "There is no one there, sir."

"Okay, thanks." Stuart hung up.

Later 0804 rang.

"Stuart?"

"Yes, Dad?"

"Hold on, I want to get your mother on the phone. Helen? Stuart's on the line."

"Hello, Stuart."

"Hi, Mom."

"I just wanted you to know that I'm home again," his father said. "Your mother and I don't want you to worry anymore."

"That's great news."

"Everything's been worked out," his mother said.

"I'm glad."

"We're sorry if we upset you."

"It's okay, I'm just happy you're back together."

Then 0802 lit up. "I have to put you on hold for a second," Stuart said. He pushed a button. "Hello?"

"Hello, Stu?" It was Carol. He felt goosebumps shoot up and down his arms and legs.

"Hello? Stu? Are you there?"

"Hi, Carol. I'm sorry, I was just a little surprised. Listen, I have to put you on hold for a second." But before he could switch back to 0804 to tell his parents he had another call, 0803 lit up.

"Hello?"

"Stu?" It was Eliot. His voice sounded weak.

"Listen, can I call you right back?"

"No, wait. We talked again last night."

"Who?"

"Carol and I."

"Where are you?"

"In a limo on JFK Boulevard," he said, his voice cracking.

"I have to call you back," Stuart said.

"No, don't, Stu. I need help, man. I'm supposed to pick up a client in five minutes, but I can't do it."

"Better pull yourself together."

"I can't. It's over, Stu, really over."

"I thought you knew that."

"I knew it was temporarily over, but I didn't believe it

was really over. I can't make it, Stu. I'm going to kill my-self. I can't stand living anymore. Hold on." He started to cry.

Stuart held on. He imagined Eliot in one of his Paul Stuart suits in the back of a stretch limo with a color TV and bar, crying his eyes out. He didn't dare switch back to Carol or his parents for fear that Eliot would start talking again and he wouldn't be there. He could hear him sobbing.

"You still there?"

"Sure."

"Listen, I can't fuck this up. The deal is in heat and it has to close today or we'll lose it. But all I want to do is end it all."

"Stop talking that way," Stuart said in a calm, even voice like the doctors on TV. "I know it feels intolerable now, but it will get better. Have you got any Visine?"

"No."

"Tell the driver to stop at a drugstore and get some. Then fix yourself up and close the deal and call me again as soon as you have a chance."

"Aye, aye, captain." Eliot hung up.

Stuart switched back to 0802, but Carol was gone. What was the name of the company she worked for? It was right on the tip of his tongue. What a time for a mental block.

He switched to 0804. "Dad? Mom?"

"Still here."

"Hey, I'm really sorry. I had two other calls and I couldn't get off."

"It's all right," his mother said. "We understand busi-ness."

"You just keep raking it in, you hear?" his father said.

"Sure, Dad."

"And we want to know if you can come up for dinner Friday night," said his mother.

"I'll have to talk to Laurie and get back to you."

"All right," his mother said. "Try to make it. We'd love to see you and the baby."

195

Stuart hung up the phone. He really couldn't make sense of any of this.

He was staring out the French doors still trying to remember the name of Carol's company when a taxi pulled up in front of the Excelsior Arms and Charmine got out. He waited a few minutes until she got to her room and then called her.

"Hello?"

"Hi, it's Stuart from across the street."

"Oh, hello."

"I thought we were going to have lunch yesterday."

"I couldn't," she said. "I had to go downtown in the morning."

He assumed she was lying, since the Indian man had said she was out all night. But then, what made him think she owed him the truth?

"Well, how about today?"

"You're the one across the street, right?"

He'd just told her that.

"Why do you want to have lunch?" she asked.

"Well, as I told you, there are a lot of reasons. I work alone in my house and I have no one to have lunch with. And I'm curious about your life. It seems so different from the life I lead."

"Oh, I'm sure it is," she said with a laugh.

"Then let me take you to lunch and you can tell me about it."

"Oh, Stuart, I don't know."

"Listen, this is completely legitimate," he said. "I just want to have lunch. It's no big deal."

"Hmm."

"Is there a problem?" he asked. "I mean, do you have a boyfriend or someone who might get mad?"

"No."

Now 0801 began to flash.

"Can you hold a second?"

196

"Okay."

He switched to the other line. "Hello?"

"How's my Woof?" It was Laurie.

"Okay. How're you?"

"I just wanted to say I love you and that if I am pregnant I'll be very happy."

"No more Ramone?"

"Stuart . . ."

"Just kidding. I love you too, but I'm on another line."

"Don't forget to pick up Claire."

"Sure. Talk to you later." He got back on with Charmine. "Sorry, that was my wife."

"Your wife?"

"Yeah. Didn't I tell you I was married?"

"I see," she said.

"So how about lunch?"

"Call me tomorrow."

27

H E was in the kitchen making himself a tuna fish sandwich when the phone rang again. It was Eliot.

"I blew it," he said.

"How?"

"I called and said I was sick and couldn't make it."

"Okay, so they'll understand. You can close the deal tomorrow."

"There's not going to be any tomorrow."

"What?"

"It's over, Stu. I'm a fuck-up. I've always been a fuck-up and I'll always be a fuck-up. You talk about pain, man. It's not the pain of losing Carol. It's the pain of being me. Maybe I would get over Carol. But I'll always be me, and I can't take that anymore."

"Where are you?"

"Room two fifty-one, the Four Seasons."

"I should have guessed."

"Good-bye, Stu, you've been a great friend and I want you to know I appreciate everything you've done. I don't have a will but I'm leaving a note. You can have any of the apartment furnishings that belong to me. I figure I'll leave my half of the apartment to my folks."

"Listen, would you do me a favor?" Stuart said. "Would you get on the next Metroliner and come back here?"

"No."

"Then would you wait for me to drive down there? It'll probably take about two hours."

"Forget it, Stu, you can't stop me. I've got a bottle of aspirin, room service is sending up a pitcher of martinis and the Mets are playing an afternoon game at Chicago. I'm going to take the aspirin during the seventh-inning stretch and I'll be gone by the bottom of the ninth."

"What if it goes into extra innings?"

"It goes without me," Eliot said. "I love you, man. You've been a great friend. Bye." He hung up.

Stuart immediately called the Four Seasons back. "Eliot Berger's room, please."

He heard the clicks of a computer keyboard, then the operator said, "I'm sorry, we have no Eliot Berger registered here."

"Then who's in room two fifty-one?" Stuart asked.

"A Mr. Alfred E. Newman."

Stuart groaned. "Okay, please connect me with him."

"I'm sorry," the operator said. "That line is busy."

"Listen, this is an emergency. I have to know if it's off the hook."

"Just a minute please"—the operator got off and came back on—"It appears to be off the hook, sir."

"Okay, then I must get a message to the room immediately."

"I'll switch you to the concierge."

The concierge came on and Stuart gave him the message. Eliot was to call him back immediately or he would call the Philadelphia police. The concierge promised the message would be hand-delivered.

Three minutes later the phone rang. Stuart gave a silent thanks to the Four Seasons.

"What do you want?" Eliot asked.

"I want you to come back."

"No."

"Then I want you to wait until I get there."

"Maybe."

"Promise or I call the police."

"I could promise and still not wait."

"Promise me."

"Okay, I promise I'll wait until the end of the Mets game."

Twenty-eight minutes later he was driving down Eleventh Avenue toward the Lincoln Tunnel. He'd called Laurie to tell her what was going on and he'd left a message on Carol's machine at home, explaining that he hadn't called her back because Eliot was at the Four Seasons in Philadelphia threatening to commit suicide. It had taken forever to get the car out of the garage. The attendant didn't seem to believe Stuart when he said that it was a suicidal emergency and he had to get to Philadelphia fast.

"No one *has* to get anywhere fast," he replied existentially and took his time walking to the large car-carrying elevator.

But finally Stuart was on his way and the Mets were only in the first inning.

There was a fifteen-minute delay going through the tunnel and more traffic on the New Jersey Turnpike. The Mets were in the top of the third and their pitcher was giving up hits. They were going to have to bring in a reliever and he was going to have to take warm-ups. The traffic broke up and Stuart accelerated to seventy.

28

———

THE Mets were in the bottom of the eighth and Stuart was on the Ben Franklin Bridge when he realized he had no idea how to get to the Four Seasons Hotel. All he remembered was that it was off JFK Boulevard. He followed the signs.

Five minutes later he was lost. The Mets were losing by four runs. There would probably be no bottom of the ninth.

He had to stop and ask for directions twice before he found the hotel. He left his car in front and jumped out, flipping the doorman ten dollars and telling him he'd be back to park it as fast as he could. Then he ran in and took the elevator to the second floor.

A Do Not Disturb sign was hanging on the doorknob of room 251. Stuart knocked and got no reply. He put his ear to the door and listened, but couldn't hear anything. The game must have been over by now. Eliot probably wasn't even in there. He was probably down in the bar. Still, Stuart knocked again. This time he thought he heard something. It was hard to tell what. Maybe the mattress creaking or a piece of furniture being moved. He knocked again. Harder.

"Eliot, are you in there? Eliot, open up."

He heard something that sounded like a groan, then a thud, then the doorknob turned. It went left, then right.

The door wouldn't open.

"Is it locked?" Stuart asked. A pitcher of martinis. He could just imagine.

He heard scratching on the other side of the door, then a low, metallic click. The door opened and Stuart watched Eliot stagger backward, reaching for the wall to steady himself. His tie was loose and his collar open. His eyes were bloodshot and unfocused. His head bobbed on his neck unsteadily. Stuart looked past him into the room—the open armoire that housed the television, the king-size bed, the half-empty pitcher of martinis on a room-service cart.

"You okay?" he asked.

Eliot's mouth opened, but before he could speak his legs went out from under him and he slid down the wall to the floor. Stuart had never seen him this drunk, but at least he was alive. He squatted down next to him.

"Great, you've proved your point. Maybe you ought to lie down for a while until you sober up."

Eliot made no response. Stuart was worried. There was such a thing as alcohol poisoning, after all. He stood up and stepped over his friend's legs and went to look at the martini pitcher, hoping that he might be able to gauge how much Eliot had drunk. That was when he saw the aspirin bottle lying on the bed.

It wasn't a big bottle, but then, Stuart didn't know how big was big enough. All he knew was that it was empty.

He looked back at Eliot, still sitting against the wall, his eyes blank, his legs straight out on the floor. *Oh, my God . . . you dumb shit!*

He was over him in a second, hooking his hands under Eliot's arms and dragging him into the bathroom.

"You can't do this!" Stuart shouted. He turned Eliot around and picked up the toilet seat.

"*Schtop.*" Eliot fought feebly as Stuart forced his head over the toilet bowl, then straddled him from above and stuck his finger down his throat.

"You idiot!" Stuart shouted.

"*Gahrahargh.*" Eliot struggled, then gagged and puked into the toilet.

"I can't believe you!" Stuart kept his fingers in Eliot's throat. He felt the warm, slippery liquid and smelled the acrid, acid odor. God, it made him want to puke too. Eliot retched again. Stuart didn't know how long to make him vomit. He wasn't even sure how he knew he was supposed to be doing this. All he knew was that he had miscalculated. He'd underestimated Eliot's threat. What if he'd really gotten lost on the way down? Or what if he hadn't taken him seriously and had stayed in New York? He'd have Eliot's blood on his hands forever. The thought filled him simultaneously with fury and terror.

"You dumb schmuck!" He actually slapped Eliot on the side of the head.

"*Nuff . . . schtop.*" Eliot groaned. The vomiting stopped. Stuart took his fingers out. He left Eliot gasping on the bathroom floor and ran back to the nightstand to dial the hotel operator.

"Hello, operator? Listen, this is an—" Stuart stopped. On the night table next to the remote for the TV was a perfect grid of little white tablets. Six by six. "Uh, hold on a second."

He put down the phone and scrounged around for the empty aspirin bottle. The label said it contained thirty-six tablets.

Stuart picked up the phone again. "It was a mistake. Sorry to bother you." He put the phone back and sat down on the bed, staring at the empty aspirin bottle in his shaking hand. Tears came to his eyes and he started to laugh.

29

HE was sitting in the Fountain Room, eating poached salmon and wearing the jacket from Eliot's suit because the maitre d' wouldn't seat him without one. The jacket was two sizes too small and pinched terribly in the shoulders. He was certain it would split down the back before he finished his meal.

Carol walked in and stood by the doorway, looking around. Somehow, he was not surprised to see her. She was wearing a gray business suit and still clutching her car keys. Four men at a table near her stopped eating and stared. Stuart waved and she hurried toward him. He stood up and they embraced quickly.

"Where is he? Is he okay?"

"I think so. He's passed out upstairs. Just drunk."

"What happened?"

"I made him throw up. I thought he'd taken a bottle of aspirins. Turned out they were lying on the night table."

Carol seemed to relax. She gave him a funny look. "That's his jacket, isn't it?"

A fleeting drop of embarrassment trickled through him.

Stepping into her husband's clothes, huh? He grinned. "They wouldn't seat me so I borrowed it." He wasn't sure what to say next so he gestured to the extra chair at the table. "Want to sit?"

She looked at the chair. "I have to see him, Stu. It's not that I don't believe you, but I came all this way."

"No problem." He handed her the room key.

"I'll be back," Carol said.

Stuart sat down again and glanced at the table of men who'd stared at Carol. One of them winked at him. He called the waiter over and ordered an Absolut on the rocks with a twist, knowing it was her drink.

A few minutes later Carol returned and saw the drink waiting for her. "Oh, that was sweet," she said, sitting down and taking a sip.

"How is he?" Stuart asked.

"Asleep. With a smile on his face, no less. Did you prop him up on his side like that?"

"The doctor did."

"You know someone here?"

"They have a doctor on call. He came over, took his pulse, propped him up and told me to watch his breathing for an hour. He acted like it was pretty routine stuff. We checked around the room to make sure there were no other pills. I even refilled the martini pitcher and poured it off into his glass to see how many he'd had."

"How many?"

"I figure five. Six at the most. The doctor said he should wake up tomorrow with nothing worse than a bad hangover."

Carol wiggled out of her suit jacket and folded it over the back of her chair. Out of the corner of his eye, Stuart noticed that the men at the other table were watching again.

"You really thought he took the aspirins?" she asked.

"The bottle was empty. It never occurred to me to search the room. God, he scared the crap out of me. You know, I actually hit him? I mean, I slapped him on the side of the head, I was so mad."

Carol smiled sympathetically. "You're a good friend, Stu. Probably better than he deserves."

He thought about asking her what she meant, but decided not to. Carol took another sip of Absolut and looked around, adjusting to the surroundings. "I can't believe I found you. I called the hotel. They had no reservation for Eliot. Then I called Laurie and she said you'd already left. So I figured I'd take a chance and drive down." She paused and gave him a quizzical look. "I hope you're not angry."

"Why? Because you came?"

She nodded.

"No, of course not," Stuart said. He noticed that Carol was staring at his half-finished meal. "Have you had anything to eat?"

"No, and I'm starved."

Stuart caught a waiter's attention and he came over to take Carol's order. As he watched her go through the menu, he had the oddest sensation that they were behaving like slightly insane people. Two floors above, Eliot lay unconscious while they had dinner. But what else was there to do? Sit by his bedside and listen to him snore?

Carol finished ordering and smiled at him. He sensed that she felt awkward, too. Perhaps a little levity was in order. "As I drove down I kept thinking, What if there's bad weather in Chicago? What if they call the game after five innings? Eliot would kill himself on account of rain."

Carol didn't laugh. "I'm sorry, Stu. I'm still a little shaken. I don't know what I would have done if he'd really gone through with it."

Stuart took a sip of wine. "He said something on the phone this afternoon. That he was a fuck-up and a failure. Do you have any idea why he'd feel that way?"

Carol picked up the glass of Absolut and drained it, then shook her head.

206

"Did he have a couple of big deals fall through recently or something?"

She looked at him and sighed. Then shook her head again.

When her dinner came she tore apart her Cornish game hen and finished every grain of wild rice. Stuart had coffee while she ate. When she was done she dabbed her lips on her napkin and looked at him. "Do you hate me?"

"No. Why should I?"

"Because of what I did."

"I figure you must have a pretty good reason."

"I don't."

"You don't?"

Carol shrugged. "I don't know. Sometimes I think I do. And then sometimes I think I hardly have any reason at all. I don't know what's wrong with me."

"You're not in love with another man?"

"No."

"But you were sleeping—"

"I don't know why. It was something that just happened. We were attracted to each other, but he's much older and he's putting two kids through college. It was never a serious thing."

"Wasn't?"

"Wasn't. Isn't. It doesn't matter."

"But Eliot—"

"Eliot is Eliot."

"What does that mean?"

"I was his showpiece. He had to have a penthouse apartment with a great view, a BMW with a great sound system and a wife with great breasts. I was just another thing to him."

"That's not true. He's nuts about you."

"As long as my breasts don't sag and I don't get varicose veins. I told him I wanted to have a kid and he said we couldn't afford it. I told him we could move to a cheaper place and stop spending money on dumb things like fresh flowers and dinner parties. He wouldn't hear of it. I told him I was unhappy. Working means nothing to me. I don't even understand why they keep me. At least I know I'd be a good mother. Do you know what he said?"

Stuart shook his head.

"He asked what would happen if I was pregnant during the summer? Did I ever stop to think of what I'd look like in a bathing suit?"

"He didn't," Stuart said.

"I swear to God, Stu. That's when I knew. I just gave up on trying to make it work."

"And now?"

"I feel like a waif. Just floating along. You remember that Talking Heads song? '*She isn't sure about where she's gone . . . Joining the world of missing persons . . .*' I'm waiting for something to happen. I get up in the morning, put on my clothes, go to work, come home, watch TV and go to sleep. Just waiting for someone or something to tell me what to do next."

"You called this afternoon."

"Last night Eliot and I talked. He said something about suicide. I called to ask if you'd keep an eye on him"— she glanced around the room—"and I guess I wanted to talk."

"About what?"

"I don't know. About old times. I miss you and Laurie."

Stuart nodded. "Isn't there any chance of you getting back together?"

Carol shook her head. "If he was insanely jealous when he had no reason to be, can you imagine what he'll be like now?"

"Maybe he'll have to learn to trust you."

"Why? I'm not trustworthy."

"But you said this other guy meant nothing to you."

"I don't love Eliot," Carol said. "I care deeply about him, but I don't love him."

"There are other reasons to stay with him besides love," Stuart said.

"There are?"

Stuart looked at her plate. The bones were picked clean and there wasn't a grain of wild rice to be found. She was right. If you had no children and didn't love each other, what was the point?

"So what will you do now?" he asked.

"I guess I'll wait for Eliot to sue me for divorce."

"And if he doesn't?"

"Then I guess I'll sue him."

After dinner he called Laurie.

"How is he?"

"Okay. I thought he tried to kill himself, but he didn't."

"What are you going to do now?"

"Stay over and drive him back in the morning."

"Is Carol there?"

"Yes."

"What's she say?"

"She says it's over. She still cares about him, but she doesn't love him. And she misses us."

"What about the other guy?"

"She says it was nothing. Just a crush. Probably began with some harmless flirting."

"Very funny."

"How's Claire?" he asked.

"Fine. Want to talk to her?"

"No, it's okay. I'll pick her up after school tomorrow and take her to the park."

"Call me at the office when you get back."

"Why? Is something up?"

"No, I just want to make sure you're okay."

"Okay, bye."

They checked on Eliot. He was deep in martini dreamland with a steady pulse of sixty-four and rhythmic breathing.

They went down to the bar. Stuart had a Tanqueray and tonic. Carol ordered another Absolut on the rocks.

"Dave Stroud," Stuart said.

"Who?"

"Dave. He was at the party."

"Oh, right." She smiled.

"What is it?"

"Nothing. Go on."

"He was my freshman advisor at college," Stuart said. "I remember one of the first things he taught us was how to check friends' vital signs when they passed out. He also said to prop them up on their side. That way if they vomit they won't aspirate it and choke. Turned out his freshman year they had a party one night and a guy passed out. They put him to bed to sleep it off, except he never woke up."

"Oh, God."

"Have you ever had someone close to your own age die?"

"No one close," Carol said.

"Neither have I," said Stuart. "But I think about it all the time now. I mean, about Claire. I think about what would happen if she died. I don't think I could live through it. I don't think I could live without her."

"You could. My cousins's son died when he was three. About a year later they adopted two Korean kids. A boy and a girl. She says they love them like their own."

"Maybe now while they're cute and cuddly," Stuart said. "But what about when they're teenagers and they hate your guts? Won't the parents be tempted to say 'Screw it, you're not my real kid, get lost.'?"

"Some parents say the same thing to their real children."

Stuart leaned back. Carol's blouse was pulled tight across her bosom and between the buttons he could see in where the smooth skin of her breast disappeared into her skin-colored brassiere. He couldn't see more than a few centimeters of flesh, but it had the same effect as if she were sitting nude before him. He thought of Dave and Sondra. *". . . It didn't signify the beginning of a relationship. It was just something over-*

due at the end." Why did his thoughts always come back to sex? Was it just him or did every man regress to primal urges in the presence of an attractive woman? He had purposely avoided asking what her plans for the evening were, but it appeared to him now, as they ordered a second round of drinks, that she did not intend to drive back to New York.

"Has Eliot said anything about the apartment?" Carol asked.

"I think he wants to sell it."

"That's good."

"Do you think you'll get another place?"

"No."

"What about your job?"

"I'll quit as soon as everything is settled."

"And do what?"

"Go to California if nothing better comes along. Isn't that what everyone does?"

Stuart shrugged, but underneath he had the oddest sensation—as if Carol was becoming a stranger right before his eyes. As if she was no longer Eliot's wife, no longer someone whose thoughts and statements took into consideration his best friend.

"You know, this may sound strange," Stuart said. "But I feel like I'm meeting the real Carol for the first time. I mean, as opposed to the Carol who was married to Eliot."

"Do you like her?"

"Well, I think so, but it's pretty new to me."

"Hmm."

"You smiled before when I asked if you remembered Dave," he said. "Why?"

She smiled again, baring her teeth. "He was pretty bold."

"What does that mean?"

"He thought Eliot was . . . I don't know. Wimpy is probably too strong a word."

"How do you know that?"

"He told me."

211

"*He told you?* I don't believe that. Dave is a prince, a gentleman."

"Stu, when some men flirt they draw a line and you know they're not going to step over it. Other men make it obvious that there is no line. They have more than flirting in mind, but they're waiting for the woman to make the first move. Your friend Dave is definitely one of the latter."

Stuart was a bit stunned. If Dave had been that way with Carol, had he also done it with Laurie? "Did he really say bad things about Eliot?"

"No one ever says anything," Carol said. "Everything is subtle. Little hints and jabs. Dave just talked about the size of the deals he was making compared to what Eliot was doing. Not that he actually knew what Eliot was doing. But I never realized the phallic implications of a big deal."

"I can't believe we're talking about Dave," Stuart said. "I feel like this must be a case of mistaken identity."

"Is it really so shocking?" Carol asked. "Doesn't every husband lust after his friends' wives?"

"Well, uh, no. I mean, if we're talking about you, then yes, I think most men would lust after you whether they were married, single or other. But take Dave's wife, Joan. I have never found her attractive."

"All the more reason for David to be the way he is," Carol said. She finished her second Absolut. "Should we order another round?"

Stuart had not known her to drink so fervently. "We'll wind up in bed with Eliot."

Carol grinned a little sloppily. "Sounds like fun."

30

I DON'T believe this, he thought. He was sitting on the edge of the king-size bed, pulling his shoes off. The hall light near the door was on and Eliot was still asleep in the bed, snoring lightly. Carol was in the bathroom. He could hear the water running.

"It'll be like camp," she'd said.

No other rooms were available. That was, no other rooms under $250 a night. There was a perfectly acceptable hotel a few blocks away, but after their third round of drinks neither of them had wanted to go.

It'll be like camp. Not like any camp he'd ever gone to.

The bathroom door opened and Carol came out wearing a white terry-cloth Four Seasons robe.

"Are there any more?" Stuart whispered.

She shook her head. "You could call the front desk and have one sent up."

"I think they might frown on that," Stuart whispered. "Especially since neither of us is officially staying here."

Carol smiled drunkenly. Stuart got up and went into the bathroom. The bright lights made him squint. He unzipped his fly and stood at the toilet, producing a manly stream of urine. He was certain Carol could hear it. Was she impressed? Or had she heard stronger, even more manly torrents? Geysers? Porcelain-chipping water cannons?

He must have been out of his mind.

Going to bed with his best friend's wife.

And his best friend.

At the same time.

He shook himself vigorously and then washed up. Eliot's toothbrush was wet. Carol must have used it. He'd have to settle for the old toothpaste-on-the-finger routine. Finishing that, he rinsed his mouth out and dried his hands. It was time to go out. I'm going with an open mind, he told himself.

He pushed open the door.

"Turn off the light," Carol whispered from the bed.

"Then I won't be able to see," he whispered back.

"Just walk straight. There's nothing between you and the bed."

He turned off the light. The shades were drawn tightly and, true to the hotel chain's efficient manner, no stray cracks of light seeped in. Stuart took a short, tentative step.

"Carol, I think I'll sleep on the floor. This is—"

"Oh, Stu, that's ridiculous. This bed is enormous."

He sighed and took another step. It was bad enough to be in total darkness in a strange room, but he was fairly drunk too. He started to move slowly, inching each foot forward.

"How am I doing?" he whispered.

"Fine . . . I guess."

"You got the middle of the bed, right?"

"Pretty much. Eliot's taking up more than his share."

"Can't you push him over?"

"I tried, but he rolled back."

Stuart was parallel with the foot of the bed now. As he turned the corner he felt something soft under his foot. It felt like terry cloth. The robe! Jesus, she'd taken it off.

"Where are you?" she whispered.

"By the side of the bed," he answered. She couldn't see him, could she? Of course not. He couldn't even see him. What should he do now? Get into bed? With his clothes on? That was ridiculous.

He unbuttoned his shirt and threw it toward a chair. Then he pulled off his pants, folded them and dropped them on the floor. He took a deep breath and stepped toward the bed.

She'd left the blanket turned down. He slid onto the mattress and eased himself gently down until he was lying on his side. He was dangerously close to the edge, like a mountain climber trying to sleep on a six-inch ledge. He could feel her presence behind him, her breath on the back of his neck, the slope of the mattress like a soft hill rolling down toward her.

"Do you have enough blanket?" she whispered.

"Not really." The blanket ended halfway over his shoulder.

"Here." She must have tugged some of it from Eliot because Stuart got a little more slack, enough so that he was almost covered. He slid back and was covered.

"Thanks," he whispered, wondering how close she was. He imagined her body, both with underwear and without. He was pretty certain she was lying on her side, facing him. He pictured her reaching out and drawing him close. Would he let himself go?

Eliot continued to snore. Not loudly, but more like waves crashing on a distant beach. Carol had not moved. For all he knew, she was already asleep. He closed his eyes and tried to breathe slowly. He thought he might actually be able to sleep.

Then it occurred to him that maybe she wanted him to make love to her. Maybe it was her way of saying goodbye. After all, she could have let him sleep on the floor. But would she really want to do it right in bed with her husband? Maybe she saw it as the fitting end. If Eliot always thought she was doing it on the sly, why not do it right in front of him? With the one man Eliot would never dream of cuckolding him.

But Eliot was his friend. And Carol was still Eliot's wife. Technically at least. Then again, Eliot was passed out drunk and Carol swore she'd never go back to him. And Stuart knew that when it came right down to it, there was no woman alive that he was more attracted to. Not even Charmine.

"Stuart?" she whispered.

"Yes?"

"I wanted to see if you were awake."

"I just got into bed a second ago."

Carol giggled. "I know."

Stuart lay on his side, feeling each breath he took. She wanted to know if he was awake. It was obvious why, wasn't it? It was immoral, but who was counting? It was deceitful, but you only lived once. It would betray a friendship, but at some point you had to take what you wanted. For thirty-four years he had exerted self-control, had been honest, had always tried to do the right thing. He was fair in business. He tried to be a good husband, father and provider. And a good friend.

But how many times in his life would he find himself in bed with another woman? Especially a woman as desirable as Carol? Look at it this way, he thought. A year from now, which will you regret more? Doing it or not doing it?

He rolled over. Their knees touched.

"Carol?" he whispered.

"Yes?"

"You're awake?"

"Of course."

"Carol, I've been lying here thinking and . . ." Before he could continue, he felt her fingertips press against his lips. Her skin felt cool.

"Just do it, Stuart."

31

___

HE wished he could see. Touching her in the dark wasn't the same. It was like reading *Penthouse* in braille. In the dark she was anonymous. He wanted to know it was Carol.

They kissed lightly, but quickly progressed. She must have been feeling aggressive; he liked the sensation of her hands on his body, the kisses she planted on his neck and ears. He pressed his face into her breasts, teasing with his tongue. God, he wished he could see them. He started kissing, toying, teasing the nipples until they became hard.

She was hot. Literally. Her skin was moist. It had been a hot day, and a long one. A light aroma of sweat and perfume settled around them.

He slid his leg between her knees and felt her legs part until the top of his thigh felt her dampness. He rubbed against her and she groaned and wrapped her arms around his back, pulling him down. Their mouths met again. He could feel her breasts crushed against his chest. It made him think of those inflatable rollers they use to roll boats down the beach and into the water. Rolling into the water and sailing away on a sea of lust.

Except for one complication.

His tiller wasn't working.

"What's wrong?" she whispered. She was holding him with both hands. The golf grip.

"I don't know. Too much to drink probably." He answered matter-of-factly. Like it was no big deal. Like he was utterly confident of his manhood despite this minor malfunction. After all, even Ferraris ran out of gas. *But Jesus H. Christ! Why now?*

"Maybe you need some extra coaxing." Carol ducked under the covers.

Stuart felt a hand grasp the base of his uncooperative member and a warm, moist softness envelop it. He glanced to his left and was just able to make out the dark form of Eliot motionless on the other side of the bed. I don't believe this, he thought as Carol made like he was a Tootsie Roll Pop.

It was a valiant and slurpy effort, but Stuart knew it was for naught. He couldn't do it. The alcohol was draining out of his head; he felt sober and ridiculous and a little ashamed. He reached down and pulled her up next to him.

For a while they lay in the dark, aware only of each other's breathing. Then Carol touched his face with her fingers.

"It's funny," she whispered. "This probably couldn't have happened if we didn't have so much to drink. But because of how much we had to drink, it can't happen."

"I don't know if it's that," Stuart whispered back.

"Then what is it?"

"Eliot's always been my friend. He's always trusted me. He's never done anything to hurt me. Even if my head isn't convinced, the rest of me is."

Carol was quiet for a moment. Then she said, "Stu, can I tell you something about Eliot?"

"What?"

"He's a vice-president in charge of facilities planning. The only deals he's ever made were for office furniture and computer terminals."

Stuart turned his head and tried to look at her in the dark. "What are you talking about? He flies around the country making deals."

"He flies around the country planning new retail branches in malls and refurbishing old ones."

"Why are you telling me this?"

"Because for years he's lied to you and he's made me lie too. And I just wanted you to know."

"But it's not possible," Stuart said. "Someone in that position wouldn't make enough money to—"

"I don't know where the money comes from," Carol said. "I think there's a banker at his firm who trades on inside information. Eliot finds people who will buy stock in their name and then give back some of the profits so that nothing is ever done in the banker's own name."

"I don't believe it."

"Why do you think he never sent a résumé to Dave Stroud?"

Stuart turned away. He didn't want to believe it. It was immoral, deceitful. But mostly it was so damn unnecessary.

"There's something else," Carol said.

"What?"

"When you were at Bingham, remember how he always came over to your house to watch baseball and football games? Sometimes you'd leave work papers and reports lying around. Whenever you went out of the room he'd read them."

"He could have just asked. I would have told him."

"He didn't want you to know. He always wanted to do his trades before you did yours because he could get a better price."

She was right. You didn't have to be a genius to know that big institutional moves affected the price of options. All Eliot had to do was read his stuff on Sunday afternoon and

219

then get on the phone early Monday morning and he was practically guaranteed a profit four times out of five.

So he had been deceived. And the friendship had already been betrayed. By Eliot.

Stuart lay on his back. Carol moved toward him and rested her head on his shoulder. "I'm sorry, Stu."

He didn't answer. Dave had used him as a cover for his affair with Sondra. Eliot had used him for stock tips. Was Carol using him to get back at Eliot? Jesus, was that all he meant to his friends?

He felt Carol reach toward his groin. "I thought it might have an inspirational effect," she whispered, fishing for a response.

Was he some kind of naïve buffoon? A anachronism who somehow hadn't woken up to the fact that the principal motivations of modern man were lust and greed? Was he really a fool for never using his frequent-flyer miles on his secretary and joining the Mile High Club?

"Stu?"

"I'm sorry, Carol. I guess I'm a little . . . disappointed."

She was quiet for a moment. Then she started to shift in the bed. "Maybe I should go."

"Don't," he said, feeling strangely distant. "It's not your fault."

32

HE woke up to the sensation of something crawling around his feet. It was Carol's hand. He rolled over. In the dim gray morning light she was under the blankets. A second later her head popped out. When she saw him, she smiled.

"Couldn't find my underwear," she whispered. Her breath smelled bad. The next thing he knew, she crawled over him, her ample breasts dragging across his chest one last time. She scooped up her clothes and hurried into the bathroom.

He glanced over at Eliot, still asleep on his side with his mouth open. Jesus, why did it have to be real? Why couldn't it have been a dream? He stretched and looked at his watch: 7:15. Laurie would just be waking up. Claire would be standing in her crib in her yellow Big Bird pajamas, rattling the bars and asking for muck. He missed them both.

The door to the bathroom opened and Carol emerged. She was dressed, her hair combed. He couldn't believe how fast she'd been. She walked around the bed toward him.

Stuart glanced nervously at Eliot. If he woke, he'd see her. But then, so what?

Carol kneeled by the side of the bed, her face close to his. "I'm glad it didn't happen," she whispered. "Are you?"

He shrugged. "I don't know."

She put her hand on his head and ruffled his hair affectionately. "Don't become one of them, Stu. You're so much better the way you are."

She leaned forward and kissed him, then got up. He watched her cross the room. She waved and was gone.

He heard the door close. For a second he wanted to follow her. They could run away together. Leave family and friends and a trail of crumpled spermicidal-jelly tubes scattered across the country. They'd get jobs as blackjack dealers in Las Vegas. He'd be just another guy running away with his best friend's wife. What would he lose?

Claire.

And Laurie.

No way. Not for all the tea in China. Not for all the sex in Japan. He stretched out. It was nice finally to have some room. He rolled over and went back to sleep.

The sun was shining brightly over Philadelphia. He and Eliot spent twenty minutes driving around downtown trying to find a pair of sunglasses. Eliot said the glare was killing him. Finally they found a drugstore. Eliot went in and came out a few minutes later wearing aviator glasses and carrying a brown paper bag.

"Home, James," he said, reaching into the bag and taking out a bottle of Pepto-Bismol and a small cellophane envelope filled with vitamin pills. As Stuart pulled away from the curb, Eliot poured the pills into his palm and knocked them back with a gulp of the syrupy pink liquid.

"God, it's great to be alive." He grinned at Stuart, his lips slightly pink.

"It's good to hear you say that."

"I wasn't talking about me. I was talking about you."

"Huh?"

"I wake up in the middle of the night and discover that my best friend is in my bed getting laid."

"Uh . . ."

"That was you, wasn't it?"

"Last night?"

"Yeah, brain, in bed, remember?"

"Uh . . ."

"You thought I was so far gone I wouldn't wake up, right? Hey, listen, you don't have to sweat it. You know I'm not going to tell Laurie. It's just good to know you're human."

"I guess."

"You guess? Where did you find her? In the bar? You didn't have to pay for it, did you?"

"Well, actually . . ."

"Aw, man, if you wanted it that bad all you had to do is drive an hour from here and you could have had all you wanted for free."

"What are you talking about?"

"Atlantic City, Stu. Any coffee shop in any casino at eleven o'clock at night. Gambling widows. Women whose husbands have told them to get lost while they gamble. Women who have had fights with their husbands over the money they're blowing. Women whose boyfriends have just disappeared. The coffee shops are full of them. And they're just waiting for someone to come along and pork them so they can have their revenge."

"Eliot, yesterday afternoon I drove down here because you said you were going to kill yourself."

"I don't want to talk about that."

"How can you not want to talk about that?"

"Shit, why don't we just go to Atlantic City now? We can play in the casinos all day and get laid tonight."

"I'm going home."

"You're no fun. For a second I thought you were human. Maybe you're only human at night. I'll have to ask Laurie."

"So help me God, Eliot—"

"I was only kidding, dummy. Anyway, was she any good? I mean, if you had to pay I sure hope she was."

"I don't want to talk about *that*."

"Hey, didn't she think it was kind of kinky, getting into bed with another guy already there? I'm surprised she didn't charge extra for it."

Keep your eyes on the road, Stuart told himself.

"Want to stop and get breakfast?" Eliot asked.

"I thought you were supposed to be hung over," Stuart grumbled.

"I'm not so bad."

Stuart stopped the car in front of Eliot's sister's brownstone on Ninety-seventh Street. His sister and her husband had bought the place about ten years before. It was the same old story. The building was now worth eight times what they'd paid for it. You probably had to go to Schenectady to find a brownstone for the same price today.

"You sure you're okay?" Stuart asked.

"Yeah." Eliot took another hit of Pepto-Bismol and rolled the top of his brown paper bag tight.

"What do you think you'll do?"

"Take a shower and go to the office, what else?"

"About things in general."

"The hell with things in general. All I know is now I have to go in and try to explain to my boss why I couldn't keep that appointment yesterday. Mental breakdowns aren't exactly the kind of ailments today's young aggressive investment bankers are supposed to suffer from."

Eliot got out, but didn't close the door. He looked back in at Stuart. "Oh, fuck it, Stu. I know it was Carol."

Stuart blinked and realized his mouth had fallen open.

"I was gonna try to pretend it was some whore so that we could still be friends," Eliot said. "But it's just piling bullshit on top of more bullshit. What did you do? Call her because you really thought I was going to commit suicide and you were hoping that she would come down and help talk me out of it?"

He nodded.

"And when you couldn't get it up, she told you I'm just a stupid fucking VP in charge of planning offices?"

"Yes."

Eliot looked down at the street. "Jesus."

Stuart turned in his seat and felt the seat belt resist. "You could've told me."

"Oh, sure. I could just see you, me and Dave sitting around shooting the shit. Dave talking about some billion-dollar hostile takeover he'd just funded. You talking about making a big score in options. And me talking about the new design scheme for the Toledo branch."

"I swear to God, Eliot, it wouldn't have made a difference."

Eliot grinned. "And I thought I was the bullshitter in this friendship."

Alternate-side-of-the-street parking was in effect and a street cleaner rumbled down the block and stopped behind them. The driver honked his horn twice, but Stuart didn't move the car. The street cleaner went around them, the driver giving Stuart the finger as he passed.

"Can I say something in the spirit of friendship I've always felt for you?" Stuart asked.

"Sure. Why not?"

"Get out of the city. Forget about investment banking. Get yourself set up in business in some warm place where you can play tennis and chase girls. You don't need this crap."

Eliot nodded. He was quiet for a moment. "Think you'll see Carol again?"

"No."

"Did she say what she was going to do?"

"She said she was going to let the wind blow her wherever it wanted. And if it didn't, she'd probably go to California."

"Funny, that's where I was thinking of going too."

"Do it."

Eliot reached into the car. It took Stuart a moment to realize he wanted to shake hands. "No hard feelings, okay? We each did what we had to do."

"Sure." Stuart put the car in drive and pulled away from the curb. He felt ashamed, felt like he'd hit Eliot in his most vulnerable spot when he least needed it. He'd been wrong last night. A year from now he would not regret that he hadn't slept with Carol. A year from now he would regret what he'd done to Eliot. Suddenly he knew what his father had meant the night they'd strolled down Columbus Avenue. Sharks always went for injured prey. He had become a shark without realizing it. Well, at least now he knew.

As he turned the corner, he looked in the rearview mirror and saw Eliot standing on the sidewalk, watching him. Damn it all, Stuart thought. Damn it, damn it, damn it.

33

LAURIE was pregnant.

"How?" Stuart asked once they'd calmed down.

"Diaphragms are only ninety-eight-percent effective."

"Are you happy?"

"Yes," she said. "Are you?"

"I will be if you promise me it's mine."

"Stuart . . ."

"Just tell me."

"It's either yours or God's."

"Uh . . . I think that's okay."

"I'm going to quit," Laurie said.

"When?"

"As soon as it can be done in an orderly fashion."

"You sure?"

"Very," she said. "As long as we can afford it."

"I'll make a few calls."

Three days later 0802 rang.

"Time to have lunch." It was Dave.

"What's the offer?" Stuart asked.

"Two and a quarter."

"Vacation?"

"Sure, all the vacation you want, except you'll never have time to take it."

"I guess I'll have to take my suits out of storage."

"You are incredibly smug."

"Just well taught."

"Be at Delmonico's tomorrow at twelve-thirty," Dave said. "Jamison will be there to make it official. And do me a favor, try to appear grateful."

Stuart smiled. "I am."

34

H E stood by the French doors, resting. All morning
he'd been packing up files, making phone calls,
getting his business in order. He wasn't even
thinking about Charmine. Her shade was pulled down, but
he gazed up at it anyway, his mind adrift. He'd had lunch
with Jamison a week ago. This was his last day home. Tomorrow he'd be back at Bingham.

He had not heard from Eliot or Carol. He knew from a
neighbor in real estate that their apartment was on the market. He kept thinking about calling Eliot, but he couldn't.
He knew he would someday, but it might take some time.

And Carol? She was out there somewhere, wanting what
he and Laurie had—a marriage, a family, a sense of sta-
bility. Thinking back to their night at the Four Seasons, he
was glad that they had not made love. On subsequent
nights with Laurie he found himself fully operational, so he
didn't have *that* to worry about.

He thought about names for the new child. If it was a
boy, he was leaning toward Sean. For a girl, he liked Sarah.
He wanted to turn the office into a den, but Laurie was

campaigning to break down the wall and expand the living room.

Suddenly across the street the shade shot up as if someone had started to raise it and then lost their grip. Charmine stood at the window, stark naked, her mouth agape with surprise.

She saw him and he saw her. Her right arm slowly rose to cover her bare breasts, but instead of scurrying away, she stood still, a smile curling her lips. He raised his hands to shoulder level and shrugged as if to say, "What can you do?"

Her smile grew wider. She reached up to the shade with her left arm, standing on her tiptoes. For the first time he saw the dark hair below her belly. A second later the shade came down.

He called the hotel and asked for her room.

"Hello?"

"Hi, it's Stuart. The guy across the street."

"I knew it was you. So would you like to come over?"

The question went through him like electricity. "Well . . ."

"Really, Stuart, let's get to the point. You can come over. Isn't that what you really want?"

"Well, uh, I uh . . . You mean, come over now? Just like that?"

"Since I hardly know you, perhaps it would be nice if you brought a gift."

"A gift?"

She sighed. "Think it over for a moment, darling. I'm sure it will start to make sense." She hung up.

It made sense. In fact, it was what he had suspected all along. He was just surprised that she'd been so forward about it. Then again, it was business. As in investment banking, she offered a service in what was no doubt a competitive market. You didn't get clients by waiting for them to come knocking. You went out and, excuse the expression, "hustled."

He imagined her slender figure and olive skin. Her body would be firm, her imagination lively. He could picture them making love on the floor of her sun-splashed room. They'd purposely leave the shades up so that all the other guys on his side of the street could see.

He turned from the window. It was an amusing thought, but he still had a lot of packing to do. That night he was taking Laurie out to celebrate. Tomorrow he was going back to work. They were going to have a new child. And more than ever, he felt like a family man.